CHILDISH THINGS

Robin Jenkins

CANONGATE

First published in Great Britain
in 2001 by Canongate Books Ltd,
14 High Street, Edinburgh EH1 1TE

Copyright © Robin Jenkins 2001

The moral rights of the author have been asserted

British Library Cataloguing-in-Publication Data
A catalogue record for this book is
available on request from the British Library

ISBN 1 84195 122 6

Typeset by Hewer Text Ltd, Edinburgh
Printed and bound by CPD, Ebbw Vale, Wales
www.canongate.net

In memory of my mother

'When I became a man I put away childish things'

PART ONE

1

Let's admit it, in all our activities, golf and war, politics and religion, there is an element of childishness. Truly adult persons are as rare as saints. There was only one at the grave that sunny September afternoon: the woman in the coffin, my Kate, dead from cancer, bravely and humorously endured.

Take the minister, the Rev. Dugald Abercrombie, white-haired and gaunt, with an involuntary girn in his voice. After half a century of having his exhortations politely disregarded, he could not help sounding disappointed and a little resentful. His joints were inflamed and painful with rheumatism. He had lost his own wife eight years ago. He thought he had deserved better, like a child that had always done what it was told. God, the Father, had let him down.

There was Kate's brother, Hector of the doleful countenance. Fifty or so years ago, he had gone to prison rather than be sent to war. No man ever knows exactly his own motives, but surely Hector – absurd name for a pacifist – must have been deceiving himself when he had declared, unavailingly as it turned out, that, by refusing to kill the persecutors of the Jews, he had been benefiting all humanity. Nowadays he lived alone with a horde of cats and kept a second-hand bookshop that seldom had customers. Looked at in one way, his qualms were noble, but looked at in another way, childish. Really, as I had once pointed out to him, he had spent his life in a puerile huff. Even Kate, most loving of sisters, had been impatient with him at times. He was missing her, though. Those tears were genuine. I loved him for them.

There was Henry Sneddon, who had vowed never to speak to Hector, in this life or in any other life there might be.

I had often rebuked him for what I called his unsoldierly lack of generosity. So had his wife Helen, most forgiving and least embittered of women. He was greatly dependent on her. At present, there she was, holding him up, though, at 78 she was a year older. Once, with great tenderness, she wiped his face, of slavers I thought, uncharitably, but it could have been tears; he too had been fond of Kate. No doubt Helen had arranged for him to use the minister's private toilet in the kirk, if need be. Poor fellow, he claimed that his incontinence was the result of his having taken part in the Normandy landings 40 years ago.

There was Susan Cramond, in her £1000 fur coat. A wealthy widow only a few weeks from her 70th birthday, she did cycling exercises, dieted, swallowed vitamins by the handful, consulted astrologers, wintered in the Bahamas, and bribed God with large donations to the church, all to fend off the old skinny fellow with the sharpened scythe. From the other side of the grave, she was gazing at me, in childish appeal. Would I, please, would anyone, save poor Susan? She had, I may say, a reputation in the town for being hard of head and heart. Could it be that she was afraid of hell, though outside the graveyard she'd scornfully tell you she didn't believe in it?

There were the Tullochs, Millie and Bill, she gazing up at him with cowlike meekness, he ignoring her as he so often did; he was usually punishing her for God knew what. At 55 or so, they were a good deal younger than the rest of us. Millie was present because Kate had been kind to her, Bill because he made a hobby of attending funerals, not because he wanted to share people's grief but because he enjoyed it. I didn't like him, even though I sometimes played golf with him.

Millie had a small doll-like face, with voice to match, thin and rather shrill. She had also, disconcertingly, one of the roundest, most enticing dowps I had ever seen. She showed it off to its best advantage by wearing her skirts and trousers too tight. Some thought she was being naive and guileless; others, including me, weren't so sure.

There were my daughters, Madge and Jean, quietly weeping. They loved me and I loved them but now and then they gave me sad, reproachful looks. They thought that I had not appreciated their mother as I should. It was true and it broke my heart. But who is ever valued as he or she deserves? We leave that to God, whether we believe in Him or not.

Present also were Alec Riddick, one-time Sheriff; Angus McVey, ex-lawyer; Archie McBain, retired civil engineer; and Jimmy McDowall, quantity surveyor, also retired: all septuagenarians and citizens of substance. They, with Henry if his bowels allowed, met with me every Tuesday morning in Murchison's tearoom in the main street, where we discussed the affairs of the world, often with, I have to confess, childish clamour. We had done it for years. It was an institution in the town. Outnumbered, for they were all Tories, I kept my end up with much wit and a little sophistry. At Armistice time they wore their medals. I could not, for in my case it would have been showing off. I had won the Military Medal and could claim to be a hero.

Then there was myself, Gregor McLeod, 72 years of age. What was it Kate had said, with affection, but also with her elusive irony that so often had me searching? 'But, Gregor, how could you teach primary schoolchildren for forty years and not acquire some of their characteristics?' She was right, of course. My pride in my collection of books, my red Mercedes with the black leather upholstery, my Ping golf clubs, and my wardrobe of expensive blazers and tweed suits was akin to that of a small boy in his comics, his bicycle, and his Rangers strip. In my favour I could claim that I knew my faults, as a shepherd knows his sheep, and rounded them up from time to time to dip them in the disinfectant of self-criticism.

As the handfuls of earth were dropping on the coffin, I was in

5

tears. 'Dear Kate,' I murmured. If the minister was right and the dead – so he had seemed to say – shared God's knowledge and therefore knew everything, then Kate heard and saw me. I imagined her smiling. She had had the loveliest of smiles. She had it when she was 24, at the time of our marriage, and she still had it when she had died, 46 years later.

Crows cawed overhead, but not in derision.

2

After the funeral, Madge and Jean sought me out in my study, where, to tell the truth, I was looking at photographs of Kate. They wanted to know my plans for the future. They had promised their mother that they would look after me.

Kate must have been much amused.

Madge, aged 45, was tall and fair, like her mother in appearance. She had an honours degree in Economics. Her views were right-wing. She had met her American husband Frank in London, where they were both working, she at the Treasury and he at the British branch of his Californian bank. They had a son and a daughter. Madge had acquired a transatlantic drawl.

'Dad, Madge and I would like to know what you intend doing,' said Jean, her eyes still red from weeping. 'We know that you think you can look after yourself. Perhaps you can now but soon you'll not be able to.'

'We don't think you should stay on in this house,' said Madge. 'It's too big. You'd feel lonely. You'd be haunted by memories of Mom. You'd be happier in a small flat downtown.'

'You wouldn't need a car if you lived there,' said Jean. 'You could walk to anywhere you wanted. You could take a taxi to the golf club, But in any case you'll soon have to think about giving up golf.'

It was time to torpedo this well-meaning but mistaken solicitude.

'I'm thinking of going to India,' I said.

'India!' they cried, aghast.

'Where the Taj Mahal is.'

That magnificent monument to a beloved wife.

'To one of those ashrams?' said Jean.

'Yes, Jean, to an ashram.'

'Are you serious, Dad?' asked Madge.

Well, was I? I had good reason to be serious. I had just lost the woman I had been married to for 46 years. In an ashram, where humility was encouraged, I might be better able to cope with my grief.

'I've read about them,' said Jean. 'Frauds, many of them. Always on the look-out for gullible old fools who'll give them all their money.'

'Thanks very much, Jean,' I said.

'But, Dad, you've never been religious. You used to grumble when Mum let us go to the Sunday school.'

'I was young then and prejudiced.'

Madge then spoke, or rather, made an announcement. 'If you feel the need for the comfort that religion can give, you do not have to go as far as India to find it.'

Jean, sly besom, then hit on what she considered an incontestable argument. 'You'd have to shave off your hair and your moustache.'

She knew I would never sacrifice my abundant, wavy, snow-white locks and moustache to match for all the gurus in India.

Madge had another announcement to make. 'You may like to know,' she said, haughtily, 'that Frank and I recently gave ourselves to Jesus.'

I was horrified but not surprised. I had met the minister of their local church in San Diego: a fat, bald, evangelical clown, who kept crying, 'Hosannah!'

Jean took the news coolly. 'That's your privilege, Madge,' she said.

Just then, Frank, straightening his black bow tie, came into the study to say in his soft voice that the taxi to take him and Madge to the airport was at the door. He had already shaken my hand, soulfully, at least eight times in the past three days, but he did it again.

'I hope Madge has told you, Dad,' he said, 'that you will be very welcome in San Diego if ever you should choose to pay us a visit.'

'Robert and I will always be glad to see you in Edinburgh,' said Jean.

'They often ask about you at the Country Club,' said Frank. 'Don't they, Madge?'

Madge did not answer.

'Mrs Birkenberger – you remember her, Dad? – asked me just the other day when you were coming back.'

'Didn't she used to be the actress, Linda Blossom, in black-and-white films?' said Jean. 'Married and divorced four times.'

'Five' said Madge.

'But she's very very rich', said Frank, fervently. 'Our bank handles a lot of her affairs. She owns the land on which the Country Club is situated.'

'And she thinks it gives her a right to behave disgracefully,' said Madge.

I well remembered the redoubtable Mrs Birkenberger. As Linda Blossom, she had been an internationally famed beauty. I had met her at the Poinsettia Country Club. Impressed by my graceful golf swing, and by my ducal demeanour, she had invited, or rather, commanded me to play a few holes with her. I had enjoyed it, though she had played very badly and used language unfit for a golf course. 'Fuck it!' she had cried after every duffed shot, and there had been many. Afterwards, members had whispered congratulations into my ears. I had been in a cage with a lioness of unreliable temper and had emerged unscathed. She was small and stout, with her face heavily made up and her hair dyed jet black. She had laughed often and randily. It was rumoured that she hired young athletes to pleasure her in bed. I hadn't been attracted to her sexually, thinking her too old and uncouth, but I had had Kate to be faithful to and keep me in line. It could be different now. If, after a lifetime of sleazy amours, the lady was looking for a mature gentleman, cultured, handsome, witty, knowledgable, and (fingers crossed) an able enough lover, given the right encouragement, why shouldn't I toss my Panama into the ring?

As for Kate, she, good sport, herself out of the game, would cheer me on. Hadn't she, on her death-bed in the hospital, too weak to wink, whispered that I was not to grieve too long but was to try and enjoy what little was left of my life?

Some may think me a monster, one minute talking of retreating to an ashram, and the next dreaming of a dalliance with a foul-tongued elderly millionairess. But that is how human beings are. No one is surprised to learn that the keeper of the gas chambers was a loving husband and indulgent father.

3

When they were all gone I wandered about the house, touching things that Kate had touched and looking at photographs with her in them. There was one when she was young, smiling fondly. Who is she so fond of? Whose arm is she holding? It is a young soldier, in the kilted uniform of the Argylls, with the ribbon of the MM on his chest. It's me, more than 40 years ago: the moustache is black. I look upwards, as if I had high ambitions. Yet, when the war was over, I returned to being a primary schoolteacher. It was a safe, worth-while job, and I had two small children, but it fell far short of what I thought my talents deserved. True, I rose to be headmaster of a large school, I became influential in educational circles, in spite of being a member for a while of the ILP, and I always did well in the Scottish Amateur Golf Championship, once reaching the quarter-finals. Latterly, Susan Cramond, who was a friend of the Lord Lieutenant of the county, had suggested putting my name forward for an OBE for services to education.

There was an apron of Kate's hanging on its usual hook in the kitchen. Madge and Jean must have overlooked it when getting rid of their mother's clothes. I pressed it against my face.

Despair crept near, but was I capable of genuine despair?

Suddenly it came to me that there was one person I had never taken in. I had last seen her at least ten years ago. We had parted in anger. I had called her a slovenly bitch, she had called me a fraud. She might be dead, for she had had a tendency to become

11

fat and was a heavy smoker, but I felt a desire, a passionate need, to go and find out.

Her name was Chrissie Carruthers. She lived in Gantock, 15 miles along the Firth. I could hardly call her my ex-mistress for I had never spent any money on her and had been to bed with her once only. It hadn't been a success. She had laughed and quoted Plato, and her feet hadn't been clean. A common interest in literature and politics had brought us together. We were both members of the ILP. In spite of painful feet, she had gone on marches against the Bomb and other abominations of our time, while I had stayed away, using the argument that such demonstrations were never effectual, but really, as Chrissie had pointed out, because I thought them vulgar, with their silly banners and idealistic optimism. If she was alive, was she still politically active? Did she still have the portrait of Rosa Luxemburg on her mantelpiece?

I would go and find out. I might look in on Hector too.

It was dark as I drove alongside the Firth. The amber lights of Dunoon twinkled across the water and, every five seconds, there was a flash from the Toward Lighthouse. If any of my Lunderston acquaintances recognised my Mercedes, they would think I had come out for a drive, being unable to settle in the empty house. If they had ever heard of Chrissie, it would have been as Miss Carruthers, eccentric teacher of English in Gantock High School.

The west end of Gantock is a district of wide tree-lined avenues and big stone villas built in Victorian times, when there were no motor cars. Most, therefore, had no garages, so that cars had to be left out in the street. I parked mine, not in Chrissie's avenue, but in the one next to it. There was no need to be apprehensive about leaving it unattended. Police cars frequently patrolled that area of high ratepayers.

As I walked to Chrissie's, I met no one. I saw a cat. Perhaps it was one of Hector's on the prowl. He lived close by.

Most of the villas being too big for single families to maintain, they had been divided into flats. Chrissie's was on the ground floor. Furtive as Troilus sneaking past the Greek sentries, I went through the gate and up the short flight of steps. Careless as ever, Chrissie had left the outer door open. The inner door of frosted glass showed a light in the hall. I rang the bell.

She still lived there. On a small brass plate was the name C. Carruthers.

She came shuffling to the door – so her feet were still sore – and opened it without hesitation. Her spectacles were pushed up onto her hair, which was almost as white as mine but as unkempt as ever. She reached forward to peer at me. There was a cigarette in her mouth and a smell of whisky off her breath. She was wearing a long green skirt and a red woolly jumper, fastened at the neck by a large safety pin. Her colour hadn't improved and the shadows under her eyes were almost black.

She took the cigarette out of her mouth. 'Why, Gregor, it's you,' she said, as if unsurprised.

'What's left of me, Chrissie. How are you?'

'Fatter, as you can see, and my feet are still killing me. *You're* looking grand.'

She must have meant the blue blazer with the gold buttons, and the white cravat. Surely she wasn't too myopic to see the grief on my face.

'Come in, Gregor.'

'Thank you, Chrissie.'

As I followed her, I saw that her bottom had got bigger and more shapeless. 'It never bothers me, Gregor,' she had said. 'I just sit on it.'

In the living-room, on a table in front of the gas fire, were exercise books, a glass with whisky in it, a box of cigarettes, and an ash-tray. When I was headmaster, I had objected to members of my staff marking, drinking, and smoking at the same time.

That I had done it myself before my elevation had been beside the point.

'Make yourself at home,' she said.

She took my hat and threw it at a sofa. It landed on the carpet among books and newspapers.

'Would you like a cigarette?' she asked.

'No, thank you, Chrissie. I gave it up years ago.'

'Is that why you're looking so spry? What about a dram then?'

'A small one, please. I'm driving.'

Glasses in hand, we stared at each other.

Tears came into my eyes. This was unwise, in that company, this was the woman who had called me a fraud, but I could not help it. They were as genuine as my nature allowed.

'So your wife's dead,' she said. 'I saw the notice in the *Herald*.'

'Kate was buried this afternoon.'

'I'm sorry, Gregor. Cancer, was it?'

'Yes.'

'Her brother told me.'

'Hector?'

'I go into his shop now and then to buy a book.'

'You must be the only one who does.'

'Yes, he's not very busy. I met her just the once. I liked her. She had a merry laugh.'

'Yes, she had.'

'I hope she didn't suffer.'

'She did, a bit, at the end, but she bore it bravely.' My voice trembled.

'Poor soul.'

Then we sat in silence for a minute or so.

'You've lost no time in coming to ask me to take her place, Gregor. I'm afraid I can't accept but I appreciate it just the same.'

This was Chrissie's not very subtle irony.

'I'll never marry again, Chrissie,' I said. 'No one could take Kate's place.'

14

'If anyone does, she'll be younger, bonnier, tidier, thinner, and richer than me.'

She had often poked fun, with a tinge of contempt, at my ambition to be rich. After all, I was supposed to be an egalitarian. But she was not to know, for I would never tell her, that what I really wanted was to be in a position one day to exorcise memories of childhood, when I had been so often, so bitterly, degraded by poverty.

Not even Kate had known about that.

I said, 'My daughter Madge and her husband want me to go and live with them in San Diego.'

'Why don't you? Best climate in the world, they say.'

'And sunshine is kind to old bones.'

'Lots of rich old widows.'

'Why not? Look what money can buy.'

'Swanky cars. Swish blazers.'

'And books. And theatre tickets. And travel to exotic places. And immunity from the insolence of inferior men.'

She laughed. 'Who ever dared to be insolent to you, Gregor.'

'There was a time, Chrissie.'

'You're not going to tell me about it?'

'No.'

'Well, would you like us to read something suitable? *Adonais*? *Urn Burial*? *Ecclesiastes*?'

'You've got those essays to correct.'

'I'll finish them later. It's a waste of time anyway. They pay absolutely no heed to my corrections and suggestions.'

As a teacher, I had had similar doubts about the value of homework but, as a headmaster, I had had to insist that every class got plenty of it.

There was no sign of the portrait of Rosa Luxemburg, the German pacifist and socialist, murdered by evil men. Chrissie's ambition had been to write a book about her.

15

What had happened? I did not ask. If her dreams of a juster world had faded, it was not for me to crow.

'Are you going to pay Hector a visit while you're here?' she asked. 'He's not well.'

'He looked very ill at the funeral.'

'He was fond of his sister.'

'He didn't visit her very often. I suppose that was because of me. Yet I never did him any harm.'

'He thought you weren't fair to your wife.'

An opinion, it seemed, shared by many. If they were right, it was too late to make amends. I felt desolate.

'Were you unfair to her, Gregor?'

'You'd have given me six-and-a-half out of ten, Chrissie.'

'What would she have given you?'

I heard Kate's voice. It's no business of hers, Gregor. Tell her ten.

It was the kind of question typical of Chrissie. Even at 60 or so, she still put truth, as she saw it, before compassion.

'What are we heathens to do, Chrissie, if we feel we deserve divine punishment but there's no God to inflict it?'

'If I was God, I'd punish no one.'

'Not even the exploiters of the poor? The supporters of the Bomb?'

'You should go to California, Gregor. You'd be in your element there.'

'Because I'm a determined individualist?'

'Because you're a fraud. But then, we all are, aren't we? You do it with more style than the rest of us.'

'I loved Kate.'

'I'm sure you did, Gregor, in your own way. But who am I to talk? I don't think I've ever loved anyone in my life.'

'That's a terrible thing to say, Chrissie.'

'Is it?'

'You've spent your life loving the poor.'

16

'Being sorry for them. I can't claim to have loved them.'

'Have you given up politics then?'

'I don't go to meetings, if that's what you mean.'

I stood up. I picked my hat off the floor. 'I'll see myself out.'

'No. I'll see you out. It might be the last time.'

In the hall, she gripped my arm. 'I'm sorry, Gregor, if I've hurt your feelings again.'

I patted her hand. 'I think I came to have my feelings hurt. Good for me, Chrissie.'

At the door she said, 'Good luck,' and added, 'with the rich old widows.'

'Good luck to you, Chrissie.' Perhaps, before she died, she would find someone to love.

I wanted to be at my most dignified as I went out but I missed a step and stumbled.

'What do you wash your steps with, Chrissie?' I asked.

'I can't remember when I last washed them.'

'They should be washed regularly. Wet moss can be slippery.'

Like human relationships, I almost added.

4

Hector's house was in darkness. Though it wasn't yet nine o'clock, he would be in bed. God knew what dreams he had. It had been his and Kate's family home and had been left to them jointly. A large stone villa with an extensive garden, it was worth a great deal of money. Kate's share would now be mine.

Their father had been a popular philanthropic doctor, with most of his patients among the poor in the east end.

I kept my finger on the bell-button, though I wouldn't have been surprised to know that it didn't work. The whole house was decrepit, the garden was a jungle for cats. Kate had refused to put pressure on her brother.

A more brilliant scholar than ever I was, with a first-class degree in Classics, Hector after the war had, perversely, continued to work as a farm labourer until his strength ran out. He had then bought the bookshop. He had once cast up that the war had been good to me. Millions had been slaughtered so that I could win a medal and use it to rise in my profession, while he weeded turnips.

At last noises were heard behind the door.

'Who's there?' It was Hector's sullen defeated voice.

'It's me, Gregor.'

'What do you want?'

'To talk to you, about Kate.'

'I don't want to talk to you. Go away.'

I couldn't resist being sarcastic. 'I thought, Hector, your sympathies were with poor suffering humanity.'

'When did you ever suffer?'

'I'm suffering now. I loved Kate.'

'You've never loved anyone but yourself.'

This was a man I had tried to be friendly with, whose stand as a conscientious objector I had defended. But I kept my temper. A winner of the Military Medal ought not to let himself be provoked by a querulous failed peace-monger. Besides, at the graveside he had wept.

'For Kate's sake, Hector, open the door.'

Under my breath I sang a snatch of Burns's poignant song: 'Oh open the door, some pity to show.' I had sung it at Burns suppers. On the other side of the door was a man who had never been at a Burns supper in his life.

His opening of the door was a lengthy business. Two keys had to be turned, a bolt withdrawn, and a chain removed. Hector, when revealed, was carrying an ebony baton.

This was a man supposed to trust in the goodwill of neighbours and nations.

Even as a boy, according to Kate, he had never taken part in children's games. In the greatest game of the century he had refused to participate and so had missed the immeasurable joy of sharing a noble and dangerous cause with many comrades.

The hall stank of cats' piss. A big ginger Tom was on top of a small white female, clutching her with his claws. On his face was an expression of single-minded dedication that no human lover could ever have achieved.

'What do you do with all the kittens?' I asked.

'I give them to children.'

'What about those you can't give away? Do you drown them?'

He didn't answer.

The living-room was even smellier. Every chair was occupied by a cat. I threw one off and sat down. I held my hat on my lap.

This was to keep cats off. Two were already nudging against my legs.

Hector was wearing an old dirty dressing-gown over his pyjamas. He seemed reluctant to put down his cudgel. I kept on the alert. This stench might have a murderous effect, like a drug.

'You knew Kate a lot longer than I did, Hector. You were both born in this house.'

He had a face like a medieval martyr, with sunken cheeks, morbid eyes, and invisible thorns on his brow. He had taken it all, life and death, too seriously. He had never hurt a fly and yet he still agonised in his conscience more than men who had bombed cities. He was proof that no one could be at home in the 20th century who wasn't prepared to kill his fellow men, let alone drown kittens.

As far as I knew, he had never had a girl-friend. That was another game he had kept aloof from. It was a wonder he hadn't had all his cats neutered.

I was already regretting that I had come. The room was poorly lit. Was that a photograph on the sideboard? Yes, it was. She was smiling. Where are you, Kate, my love? My eyes were wet.

'Madge said you might be going to live with her in California,' he said, craftily.

'They've invited me. I haven't decided.'

'Oh, you will go. You will be in your element there.'

Chrissie had said that too. They must have been discussing me in his forlorn shop among the unsaleable books.

'You will do what suits you,' he said. 'You always have.'

'Don't we all?' But it was useless trying to joke with him.

'You more than most,' he said.

That accusation of selfishness was hard to take from a man who had put his own piddling little conscience before the saving of civilisation.

'Even your own daughters distrust you.'

Though I was sure it was a lie, I was hurt and angered.

Of course, they had always preferred their mother to me, but they hadn't given her all their love and trust. There had been some left for me.

'When they were children, they had to go without so that you could swagger about in expensive clothes.'

'Who told you that?'

'Kate told me.'

If he had driven a dagger into me, I couldn't have been more wounded. I didn't believe him, but the very insinuation that Kate had denigrated me behind my back was unbearable.

There had been a time, after the war, when we had found my teacher's salary insufficient, but Kate had seen to it that the girls had not suffered.

'She didn't trust you either,' he said.

Well, did she? Completely? Did any human being ever trust another completely? Yes. I had trusted Kate completely.

'Did she tell you that she was leaving her share of this house to me, not to you?'

No, she hadn't told me.

'I intend to leave it to the SPC.'

'What's that?'

'The Society for the Protection of Cats. I have more respect for cats than for my own kind.'

I felt like heaving a cat at him but instead I was witty. 'They've certainly got more dignity.'

Even when committing rape or incest, they looked dignified.

'She never forgave you for all those women.'

'All what women?'

In 46 years of marriage I had been unfaithful to Kate only once: Chrissie Carruthers didn't count. In Egypt, during the war, a thousand miles from home, and the girl, dark-skinned – what was her name? – had been made to understand from the beginning that she could never take Kate's place.

I had often thought of confessing to Kate, but shame had prevented me.

I couldn't deny that I was attractive to women. I knew what to say to them. They enjoyed my company. Kate had been amused but never jealous. She knew that I exalted her above them all.

'You're ill, Hector,' I said. 'You should see a doctor.'

His illness – was it cancer too? – had brought out his strong resemblance to his sister.

I stood up and put on my hat. Two cats impeded me. I felt like kicking them, to get revenge on their owner, but instead I bent down and stroked them.

'Good night, Hector,' I said, and left.

5

Some weeks later, a few days before I was to fly off to San Diego, Susan Cramond telephoned.

'I'm thinking of giving a little farewell dinner party for you, Gregor.'

'That's very kind of you, Susan.'

'You don't sound very enthusiastic.'

Well, what did I have to enthuse about? I was an old man who needed to piss oftener than was convenient or seemly. I had had my innings and, though I had performed with some style, I hadn't scored all that highly, except perhaps for my Military Medal. My wife had died recently and I was finding out every day how much I had depended on her. I was afraid that my going to California might turn out to be a mistake. I kept thinking that I should have gone to India, to an ashram, where I could have mourned with honourable resignation and found forgiveness.

It was myself I had to forgive.

'Who would you like me to invite?' asked Susan.

Ignoring Hector's opprobrious visage, I would have liked to nominate Mrs Cardross, manageress of Colquhoun's licensed grocer's in the main street. Why? Because she reminded me of Kate when Kate had been young: tall, fair-haired, blue-eyed, smiling, gracious. But of course it was out of the question even to mention her name.

'I suppose the usual bunch of boring old buggers,' said Susan. 'You can't have the Tullochs, though. They're scored off the list.

He is anyway, and she wouldn't come without him, the silly cow. To tell you the truth, it's really her I can't stand, flashing that arse of hers in every man's face.'

I was dismayed. Naively I had assumed that Millie's incomparable posterior had been admired by me alone.

'Why is Bill scored off your list, Susan?' I asked.

'Haven't you heard? It's the talk of the town. The big bull's taken his pizzle to new pastures.'

'What do you mean?'

'He's left Millie and got himself a new paramour. You must have seen her. She works in Colquhoun's, in the main street, a shop you're never out of. Fair-haired conceited bitch. She's separated from her husband. Tulloch's having to pay highly to get her to open her legs. She's driving about in a new Volvo.'

I could hardly say it. 'Do you mean Mrs Cardross?'

'That's the name. Mercenary whore.'

I could have wept. The tears would have been of self-pity and self-derision. I had been meekly content to touch Mrs Cardross's soft hand when paying for my wine and receiving my change, while Tulloch the bull had been mounting her at will.

'Does Millie know?' I asked, feebly.

'Of course Patient Grizelda knows. If you ask me, it's the best thing that could have happened to her. She should have left him long ago. So they're out. Your tearoom pals, I suppose. I hope Henry doesn't shit himself as he did last time.'

'You should insist, Susan, that we all bring our potties.'

She laughed. 'Some of us can still make it to the lavatory. I've been wondering if you'd like me to invite your brother-in-law, Hector Liddell.'

'If you did, Henry would be sure to shit himself. But why invite Hector?'

'He was at the funeral. He looked very unhappy.'

26

'He wouldn't come.'

'I suppose not. I felt sorry for him, that's all. It won't be the most thrilling of evenings, Gregor, but it'll save you the trouble of going round and saying goodbye.'

6

Next morning I hurried down to the shops, for my *Guardian*, but also to find out if what Susan had said about Mrs Cardross was true. In the main street, Helen Sneddon, in her blue Mini, caught sight of me, stopped, and called.

I went over. 'Hello, Helen. How are you?'

'To tell you the truth, Gregor, my rheumatism's so bad this morning I can hardly hold the steering wheel.'

Which would make her driving all the more erratic.

She was blocking the way. Motorists behind her tooted their horns.

'Have you heard about Millie?' she asked.

'Yes. Susan told me.'

'The funny thing is on the telephone she sounded quite excited and not a bit unhappy.'

'Surely she should be glad getting rid of a brute like Bill.'

'Yes, but can she manage on her own? She's not really grown up.'

'Which of us is, Helen?'

'That's true. These people behind me, they're like impatient children, aren't they? Did Susan tell you who Bill has moved in with?'

'Yes, she did.' I remembered the vicious description: mercenary whore.

'Mrs Cardross, who worked in Colquhoun's. Apparently she's had other men. It seems she's got an eight-year-old daughter whom she's more or less disowned. Her ex-husband has the child. What's Lunderston coming to, Gregor?'

A policeman was approaching.

'Well, I'd better get out of the way. Be sure and give my regards to Madge and her family.'

She drove off then, pretending she hadn't seen the policeman.

I walked slowly along the main street until I came to Colquhoun's, but I didn't go in. I stood with my back to it.

Passers-by who knew me – who more kenspeckle than an ex-headmaster? – nodded, smiled, and looked curious. Why was I standing there looking so wandered? I must be, they would conclude, thinking about my dead wife. Poor old bugger, they would think, what good now are his snow-white locks, his Burberry raincoat, his Italian shoes, his golf handicap of six, and his posh car? They were right, of course, but they were not to know that I had lost something more precious than all of those. Mrs Cardross, with her resemblance to Kate when young, had lifted my heart, strengthened my faith in humanity, and brightened everybody's future. Now she was revealed as mercenary, promiscuous, and heartless.

I had tears in my eyes. If they were noticed, the snell wind blowing down the main street would be blamed.

Where could I go to have faith restored? I had an idea. I would go to the school where I had been headmaster for nearly 20 years. It was interval time. I would watch the children in the playground.

As I peched up School Brae, I heard the happy shrieks of little girls. Through iron bars more suitable for a jail I peered at them, listening for the name Lenore. That was the name of Mrs Borthwick's daughter. What was Mrs Cardross's daughter called? Alas, I didn't know. I tried to look like a loving grandfather and not a potential molester, though I supposed there would be little difference as far as appearance went: in fact, the latter would probably look more benevolent. I did not hear Lenore called.

Aileen, Alison, Deirdre, and even Philomel I heard but not Lenore. There was one with red cheeks and black hair, like Mrs Borthwick. Mrs Borthwick was a waitress in Murchison's. I looked for one who resembled Mrs Cardross. There were several with fair hair.

What was it the poet Gray had written?

Regardless of their doom
The little victims play.

I felt I had to protect them all, but if I had rushed in, or rather, had clambered over the high railings, the police would have been sent for. The Sheriff would take into consideration my age, my former respectability, and my being distraught with grief. I would be given a caution, like a naughty child.

I crept sadly away.

In the afternoon I drove to the golf club to collect my clubs which were being cleaned and regripped. They were my knightly lances with which I had won tournaments. On the other hand, they were my toys, with which I played a game that, though exalted nowadays to almost a religion, was basically childish, hitting a small ball from one hole to another.

The clubhouse flag was at half-mast, signifying the death of a member. It was hardly ever at the top of the mast these days, for many members were elderly and seldom a week went by without one of them, in golfing parlance, handing in his last score-card marked 'No Return'. I couldn't think who it was this time. One day, not so far off, it would be my turn. I felt despondent. These twinges in my chest, were they caused by indigestion or incipient heart disease? And these prickles in the prostate region, were they warnings of cancer?

I sighed a lot as I drove home.

★　　★　　★

Later that day I had a visit from a young woman on behalf of the travel agency from which I had bought my air ticket. It seemed my economy-class ticket had been changed to first-class. I protested that I had not asked for such a change, which would cost a great deal of money. I was told, with a smirk, that it had been arranged by Mrs Cramond.

At first I felt insulted, or rather, told myself I ought to: how dare Susan try to buy me in this way? But, I had to ask, what possible use could she make of me once I had been bought?

I telephoned her, to remonstrate, courteously, of course, but I found myself thanking her, somewhat fulsomely. 'You deserve it, Gregor,' she said and, though I wondered what she meant, I left it at that.

To be honest, I liked very much the idea of travelling first class. Free champagne all the way. Special attention from the stewardesses. More room to stretch your legs. No queues for the toilet. A better class of passenger.

Should I accept? I already had, the ticket was in my hand, but I needed someone's assurance that I had done right.

I consulted Kate. I would never have claimed that, even after nearly 50 years of marriage, I knew her completely. There had been those silences, that elusive irony. But I thought I knew her well enough to tell what her opinion would be regarding that generosity of Susan's.

'Should I accept, Kate?'

'You already have, haven't you?'

'It's not as if I asked for it. It came as a surprise.'

'A pleasant one, though.'

'Yes, I have to admit that. After all, Kate, I'm over 70. Travelling to San Diego's very exhausting. We know that from experience. There's more room and therefore more comfort in first class. One's better able to relax. One's less likely to suffer from claustrophobia.'

I heard Kate laughing.

'Why not, Gregor?' she asked. 'Susan can afford it.'

'You're not offended?'

'Heavens, no, not a bit. Won't I be with you, in spirit? So I'll be more comfortable too.'

My Kate, my lovely Kate, my sagacious Kate.

That evening, while I was grilling chops for my tea, the telephone rang. I thought it might be Susan Cramond, but it was my daughter Jean. She had some last-minute advice for me.

'I'm going to be frank, Dad. I hope you won't mind. Robert and I are worried. You're apt to say things that upset people. For instance, you say that the Americans are more of a danger to world peace than the Russians.'

'I say it because I believe it.'

'But you don't have to say it. Especially in America. Frank may not be as smart as he thinks he is, but he's very patriotic. Remember, too, Madge is now an American citizen, and her two children, your grandchildren, are born Americans. I know it's a pose you got into years ago when you were a member of that stupid party the ILP and you've never outgrown it. You've been a bit of a hypocrite, Dad. You could never have become a headmaster if you'd stuck to your so-called socialist principles, for you must have had to do a lot of string-pulling, and toadying to councillors, and there's that bungalow of yours worth eighty thousand, and your Mercedes car, and look at the clothes you wear, the best of everything, Pringle pullovers, Daks trousers, Burberry raincoat, and sixty-pound shoes. Good for you. We'd have been the first to complain if you'd worn shabby clothes and a cloth cap and lived in a council house. We're really proud of you. But be discreet, Dad. Don't embarrass Madge. She'll have enough to contend with now that she and Frank have got religion. You won't have Mum this time to keep you in order. And, for goodness' sake, stay away from that horrible old woman Mrs Birken-

33

berger. People like her have nothing in common with people like us.'

Speak for yourself, Jean, I thought. I had quite a lot in common with Linda. She had laughed at my salacious witticisms.

'Have you got everything ready, Dad? Passport. Traveller's cheques. Air ticket.'

I could not resist shocking her. 'I'll be well looked after, Jean. I'm travelling first class.'

I heard her shrieking, 'Good heavens, Robert, he's travelling first class. But, Dad, first class is enormously expensive.'

'Well worth it, though.'

'How much did it cost?'

'Money and fair words, as your grandmother Liddell used to say.'

'Madge and Frank never travel first class on planes and he's well up in his bank.'

'Why should it bother you or her? You're not paying for it.'

'No, but we've got a right to save you from extravagance.'

I heard Robert shouting. Perhaps the length and expense of the call was distressing him.

'Robert says you could get your ticket changed back to economy and get a refund.'

'Dinnae fash, Jean. I paid for an economy-class ticket. A friend generously had it changed to first-class.'

'Some friend! Who is he? Was he at the funeral?'

'She. Mrs Cramond.'

'Is she the lady who lives in the big house at the end of your avenue? Was she at the funeral wearing that fabulous fur coat?'

'The very one.'

'Well, well. She must be rich.'

'She is.'

'I don't want to be nosy, Dad, but is there something between you and this lady?'

'What do you mean?'

34

'Well, she's old and a widow, and you're old and a widower. I'm sure Madge and I wouldn't object, so long as you waited a while.'

'But, Jean, old people cannot afford to wait, can they? Is that Robert having kittens at the cost of this conversation? Pity he doesn't have a rich admirer to pay his telephone bills. *Hasta la vista*, as they say in the whorehouses of Tijuana.'

I half-expected another call but evidently stingy Robert prevailed.

7

On the evening of my farewell dinner party I presented myself at the door of Susan's mansion, early as requested, and wearing a lounge suit, also as requested. It was opened by Mrs Borthwick, waitress in Murchison's tearoom. There was a smell of sherry off her breath. Her cheeks were rosier than ever. Her ample body exuded warmth and hospitality. What did it matter that her favourite reading was Mills and Boon romances?'

'So you're off to California, Mr McLeod?' she said, as she took my hat and raincoat. 'Aren't you lucky?'

'Thank you, Mrs Borthwick,' I said.

I had often thought of her as mistress material. She was a divorcee. Not very long ago I had given her money to buy a birthday present for her eight-year-old daughter Lenore. Kate hadn't known.

'And how is Lenore?' I asked. 'Getting on well at school, I hope.'

'Oh yes, Mr McLeod. Thank you for asking.'

It should be remembered that I had two daughters of my own who once had been little children.

'I'll send her a postcard, if you don't mind.'

'She'd like that, Mr McLeod, especially if it's one of Disneyland.'

When I came back would it be worth-while setting up a liaison with this buxom young woman? But wait, hadn't I heard that she had been seen at a dance in the Masonic Hall with a big burly bruiser called McCann? Careful, Gregor, I told myself, as I went confidently into Susan's drawing-room.

I was pouring myself a dram, malt, £30 a bottle, when my hostess came in.

'Pour me one too, Gregor,' she said.

For a woman of 70, she looked remarkably attractive. Money and a lot of time had been expended. Usually, though, she didn't give a damn how she looked. Had she made herself as womanly as possible for my sake?

She was wearing a blue dress and sapphire earrings. Her hair was blue too and had recently been permed. Her wrinkles were buried under layers of powder that had a bluish tinge. She smelled of expensive perfume.

'Remember, Gregor, after they've all gone I want you to stay behind. There's something I want to say to you.'

'By all means, Susan.' But I felt alarmed. What the hell was she up to? What did she want in return for that ticket?

The guests began to arrive. Henry Sneddon had to be cleeked from the car. There was dribble on his chin. 'I see we've got Mrs Borthwick attending us, Gregor. Gregor fancies her, you know. He pats her bottom.' Luckily, Henry's croakings were never heeded.

Considering that the combined ages of the guests were close to 1000 years, and their ailments and decrepitudes were numerous and comprehensive, the party did not turn out to be as dreary as our hostess had feared. To be fair to Susan, she helped make it a success by providing good food, mostly of a kind suitable for false or shoogly teeth, and plenty of excellent wine. With all that assortment of worn-out bladders and dodgy prostates, it wasn't surprising that there was a steady leaving of the table for short periods. Henry Sneddon had to leave twice, with Helen assisting him. Luckily he made it both times without mishap.

If I seem to make fun of old Henry, I apologise. His was a painful as well as a discomfiting malady.

The subject of the Tullochs was brought up early.

'Poor Millie,' said Helen Sneddon, and added, somewhat inconsistently, 'She's so happy now.'

'Poor Millie nothing,' said Susan, in her harsh voice. 'She should have libbed the big brute years ago.'

Susan was noted, or notorious, for plain speaking. This latest example was pondered by her guests.

'As a matter of fact,' she went on, rubbing their noses in it, 'all men, when they reach the age of fifty, should be libbed. Don't you agree, Gregor?'

Mrs Donaldson, who insisted on wearing her hat – to hide her baldness, it was thought – asked, in a thin high voice like a child, what was 'libbed'.

'You tell her, Gregor,' said Susan.

I smiled. 'That's for Bruce, surely.'

But Bruce Donaldson, Mabel's husband, like her close to 80, wasn't following the conversation. He was giving all his attention to the wine. Good for you, Bruce, I thought.

'It would prevent a lot of useless lust, wouldn't it?' said Susan, still rubbing our noses in it.

There was a rumour in the town that Albert Cramond, wealthy ironworks owner, had found Susan when she was working as a barmaid in an Edinburgh pub. No one had ever dared to ask her if it was true.

There followed a small silence.

It was broken by Jimmy McDowall, one of my 'Murchison pals'. He thought it was time he contributed to the conversation. Unfortunately, he usually spoke irrelevant nonsense and punctuated it with sly giggles. That he was 74 and therefore on the verge of dementia, might have been regarded as an excuse in other company, but not there, where most were older than he.

'This Mrs Cardross that Bill's run off with,' he said, with a typical giggle, 'is fair-haired, isn't she? Gregor prefers fair-haired women, don't you Gregor? Kate was fair-haired, wasn't she?'

They all looked crossly at him and his wife Agnes stepped on his foot under the table, but he had given them an opportunity to speak about their friend Kate.

'Kate was the nicest-looking woman I ever saw,' said Archie McBain.

His wife Sheila smiled and nodded. She was a sensible woman. There was no point in being jealous of a woman who was dead. If you were 75, there was no point in being jealous at all.

'I never heard her say a bad word about anyone.'

'She had such a merry laugh.'

'Did you ever see her dance a Duke of Perth? Light-footed as a fairy, she was.'

Yes, but not latterly. She still had danced, but not so nimbly. I felt desolate.

'It's all right, Gregor,' said Sheila McBain. 'You're not parted forever. You'll meet again in heaven.'

It would be difficult, for neither Kate nor I had been able to believe in such a place.

Morag McVey had been waiting, like a vulture, for an opening to try to ruin the party. Born and brought up in Lewis in the Outer Hebrides, she was a member of the Free Kirk. Probably she was the only person there who thoroughly believed in heaven. The rest were Protestants or Presbyterians, which meant that they did not believe in heaven (though they weren't sure about hell) or in the Resurrection, or the Virgin Birth, or miracles, but of course they still called themselves Christians.

'Gregor and Kate can never meet again,' said Morag, sternly. 'Kate is in heaven, but he will go straight to hell.'

If it had been meant as a joke, it would have been in bad taste but worth perhaps a twisted grin.

No doubt some of the guests, like myself, were reflecting that Morag's heaven would be worse than most people's hell. Nothing enjoyable would be allowed. It would be Bible-reading and psalm-singing morning, noon, and night.

'That's not a nice thing to say, Morag,' said Helen Sneddon.

I would have liked to ask the McVey bitch what she thought I had done or not done to deserve an eternity of separation and pain. There were such things, but she did not know about them. No one did. No one ever would.

'Don't heed her, Gregor,' said Helen. 'I see you as Orpheus, you know, the singer who went down into the Underworld to ask Hades the king to let him have back his wife Eurydice, who had died. He sang so beautifully that Pluto agreed, on condition that Orpheus on his way up to earth didn't look back. He couldn't resist looking back to see if she was following. She was, but she faded before his eyes and he never saw her again. What would you sing, Gregor? "Maiden of Morven"?'

That Celtic cry of anguish and longing for a dead sweetheart. It would certainly have drawn 'iron tears' from Pluto's eyes.

Henry patted his wife's hand. 'You're too old to believe in fairy-tales,' he said fondly.

Orpheus had not loved his Eurydice more than Henry with his fragile bowels did his Helen.

'But you know what happened to Orpheus,' said ex-Sheriff Alec Riddick, with a chuckle. 'He was torn to pieces by savage women.'

Somehow, that picture of me being set upon by harpies lightened the mood and cheered everybody up. Perhaps, metaphorically, they were putting their fingers to their noses at death, an ominous if invisible presence. Someone proposed that they should have a wee dance. In Susan's mansion there was plenty of room.

Susan wasn't sure, she had no objection to their dancing, but she was afraid that one, perhaps more, might drop down dead.

'Gregor's the guest of honour,' she said. 'He might not feel like dancing, considering the circumstances.'

I said that dancing was as good a way of remembering Kate as any. She had been so keen on it and had enjoyed it so much.

Anyone looking in would have been moved or amused or

41

both to see those shaky legs and gouty feet foxtrotting and waltzing, so cautiously but also so happily. No one dropped dead, though some puffed and wheezed. A Duke of Perth was recklessly demanded. If there was going to be a heart attack, it would be during that dance, however sedately it was performed. Luckily it passed off without mishap.

At last they all departed. Several offered to give me a lift home but Susan stepped in and said I ought to walk, the fresh air would sober me up.

She sat down purposefully beside me on the big couch. She smoked a cigarette, I a cigar. We both drank cognac.

'Well, Gregor, it went quite well, I suppose.'

'Very well, Susan, thank you.'

I was wondering, with some apprehension, what it was she wanted to say to me.

'That bitch McVey wasn't getting at you, you know. She was getting at me.'

'She's not worth heeding.'

'I said I had something to say to you. Well, here it is. Go to California. Get over Kate. Don't wait till March. Come back soon after the New Year. We'll go off together on a world cruise.'

In my astonishment, I let cigar ash fall onto my golf-club tie. But I couldn't help imagining myself in white slacks and nautical cap, strolling round the deck.

Would there, though, be one or two cabins?

'We're suited to each other,' she said. 'Some would say we deserve each other.'

'But, Susan, you're an unrepentant Tory and I'm a committed socialist.'

'Piffle. You're no more a socialist than I am. You're a worse snob than me. Ask anyone who knows you.'

Was that how people saw me? I remembered overhearing a remark at the golf club: 'That Gregor McLeod's a pain in the arse.' I had been captain at the time and had taken my duties seriously. If I saw a rule being wilfully broken, I immediately reprimanded the offender. It had not made me popular.

'We've got a lot in common, Gregor. We like the best of everything. We've got a guid conceit of ourselves. We like books. We like music. We like good wine. We don't give a damn who we offend.'

I winced. Was I as insensitive as that?

'As for the fucking side, we're both long past it.'

In the turmoil of emotions aroused in me, resentment surged to the top. How dare she imply that I was a eunuch, libbed by age?

'What about it, Gregor?'

'You've taken my breath away, Susan.'

'Imagine, outside the window, not the dreich wintry Firth, but the South Atlantic. Sunshine. Blue skies. Flying fish. To-morrow Cape Town. No whimpers, please, about oppressed blacks.'

'Not even a sigh or two of righteous indignation?'

She laughed. 'All right. A sigh or two. It wouldn't be you, Gregor, if you weren't allowed a dollop of humbug.'

Chrissie had called me a fraud. What they all meant, without knowing it, was that, having been born into the most dishonest, the most hypocritical century in the history of mankind, I had had to cultivate enough guile to preserve my self-respect.

'We haven't a great deal of time left, Gregor. Let's enjoy it together. I'm sure Kate wouldn't mind. She wasn't one to let death have the last word.'

Surely, if death had anything, it had the last word? But would Kate mind, wherever she was? She had always been wary of Susan.

'What would your children say, Susan?'

She had two sons and a daughter, all married. She was a

grandmother several times over. In fact she was a great-grand-mother.

'It wouldn't matter a damn what they said. Would you let your daughters stand in your way?'

I had already made it clear to Jean that I wouldn't.

'We wouldn't get married. No need for such nonsense. When we come back, you'd go on living in your place, I'd go on living here; but we'd meet more often.'

I would have dearly liked to live in her house. I coveted it. It had been built more than 100 years ago by a wealthy Glasgow merchant, and no expense had been spared, including the employment of an architect who had loved beautiful things. Everything in the house was a pleasure to see and use. Even the door knobs were things of beauty, made of porcelain with coloured pictures of elegant ladies and gentlemen in 18th-century dress. The woodwork was mahogany, the ceilings high and splendidly corniced. The staircase was palatial. In the three bathrooms, the lavatory pans were adorned with paintings of flowers. Hence, they were known as the rose lavatory, the daffodil lavatory, and the thistle lavatory, respectively.

It wasn't I, Gregor McLeod, retired headmaster, who had a great longing to live in that magnificent house. It was the small boy I had been, more than 60 years ago.

'On this cruise, Susan,' I said, 'would there be one or two cabins?'

She laughed. 'One would be a lot cheaper.'

Yes, but a lot less private. Being shut up with Susan would have its travails. Flying fish seen through the porthole would be small compensation.

'Well, Gregor, what do you say?'

'Would you mind, Susan, if I took a little time to think it over? I could give you my answer from California.'

'Please yourself. I won't see you again before you leave. I'm off to Perth tomorrow to spend a few days with my daughter Elizabeth.'

She gave me her cheek to kiss and then she telephoned for a taxi for me. I was too drunk to walk, she said.

She didn't wait for the taxi to come but excused herself and went up the grand staircase to bed.

I was much relieved that I wasn't going up with her.

The taxi-driver, it turned out, had once been a pupil of mine. He helped me into the taxi.

'Remember, Mr McLeod,' he said cheerfully, 'every Friday morning you used to give the whole school a lecture on the evils of strong drink.'

8

I was to fly off from Prestwick Airport on Saturday morning. On Thursday evening, I had a telephone call from Millie Tulloch. I hardly recognised her voice: it was still a little girl's, but not as before an ill-done-to self-pitying little girl; on the contrary, a haughty sly little girl. Pathos had suited her, haughtiness and slyness did not.

'Good evening, Gregor. Have you heard? About me and Tulloch? Of course you have. You were all discussing me at Susan's, weren't you?'

Her friend Morag McVey must have told her.

'We were all sympathising with you, Millie.'

'You needn't have bothered. I don't need anyone's sympathy. Except yours, Gregor. Yes, definitely, you're excepted.'

She giggled. It wasn't, though, like all her previous giggles, nervous and silly. This giggle had ominous purpose in it. What was that purpose?

'So you're off on Saturday?'

'Yes, Millie.'

'I hope you weren't sneaking off without saying goodbye?'

'Certainly not. I was just about to ring you when you rang me.'

'It's not the same, is it, talking on the telephone? I want you to come here and talk to me. I've got something very important to say to you.'

I was wary. 'I've not got much time left, Millie.'

'You've got tonight. I want you to come now.'

All I could think to say was 'But it's pouring rain.'

47

'Are you trying to insult me, Gregor? But I know it's not the rain you're afraid of. It's Tulloch, isn't it? Well, you needn't be. He's not here. He'll never be here again.'

'So it's finished between you and him?'

'Absolutely finished. I'm getting a divorce as soon as I can.'

'How long have you been married, Millie?'

'Thirty-four years.'

'Isn't it sad when a marriage of that length of time ends so miserably?'

'What's miserable about it? It's not a bit sad. I'll expect you in half an hour. Have you eaten?'

'No.'

I should have lied and said yes. Millie was not a good cook.

'Good. Then you can eat with me.'

Half an hour later, with rain stotting on my umbrella, as I was walking along the avenue to Millie's, I made a discovery. The prospect of being alone with her and so seeing at long last that delicious rump, perhaps in naked pulchritude, did not delight me. I was like a child who, having longed for a toy in a shop window, found, when it was in his hands, that much of its magic had disappeared.

The alacrity with which the door opened alarmed me. She seized my arm and dragged me in. This was not the timid little Millie I had known; this was a rapacious little Millie that I had never seen before. She was wearing a pink jumper and skin-tight pants that were yellow with black stripes: imitation ocelot, she was to tell me later.

To show her an example of calmness, I shook my umbrella, folded it, and placed it in the stand. Then I took off hat and raincoat and hung them up.

Impatiently she grabbed my hand. 'We'll go through to the kitchen, Gregor. It's cosier there.'

In the kitchen, a most untidy place, there was an unpleasant smell. It came from a pot on the cooker.

'What are you cooking, Millie?' I asked.

'Goulash. I'm good at goulash.'

'It smells as if it's burning.'

She laughed. 'That's a secret ingredient, Gregor. You see, I've bought wine. Is it good wine?'

There were two bottles on the table. Yes, it was good wine. My heart rose a little.

When her back was turned, I peeped into the fridge and saw cheese, cold meat, and beetroot. If the goulash was uneatable, I would still have something to eat with the wine.

She was stroking her rear. 'What do you think of my pants, Gregor?'

'Very attractive, Millie.'

'Imitation ocelot. I've got a nice round bottom, haven't I?'

'You have.'

'Susan Cramond accused me of showing it off. She was jealous. She's got nothing here at all. It's not womanly to have a skinny bottom, is it?'

'No, it isn't.'

'Mind you, I had an awful job getting into them, and I expect it'll be an awful job getting out of them, unless of course I have assistance.'

There was that giggle again.

I sat down at the table and poured wine into the two glasses. I only half-filled hers.

'More for me, please, Gregor.'

'But wine makes you sad, Millie.'

'It won't tonight, I assure you. I'm very happy, haven't you noticed? Isn't it funny, Gregor, I'm going to get a divorce and you're a widower.'

What was funny about that?

'We'll both be free.'

What was she getting at?

'Ready for your goulash, Gregor?'

'Thank you, Millie. Not too much, though. My stomach's been bothering me these last two or three days.'

'Is it nerves, do you think?'

'It could be.'

She heaped my plate with the nauseating stuff.

She sat down and ate with relish. She drank her wine as if it was water.

'Drink it slowly, Millie,' I said.

I was beginning to feel alarmed. At any moment she might break down.

'I said I had something very important to say to you, Gregor.'

Whatever it was, I tried to put it off. 'If you divorce Bill, do you think he'll marry this Mrs Cardross?'

Too late I realised that that was a damned tactless thing to say.

She answered calmly enough. I should have been warned. 'I don't care if he marries her or not. I expect he will, for he's always wanted children and I couldn't have any. Did you know, Gregor, that I couldn't have children?'

'No, Millie, I didn't know.'

To humour her, I was eating the goulash as if I liked it.

'We won't bother with them, will we, Gregor?'

'Not a bit, Millie.'

'We won't bother with anyone, when we get married.'

I was pouring wine when she said that. So great was the shock that I missed my aim and spilled it on the table-cloth. This was plastic, in green-and-white squares. I could never have married a woman that put a plastic cloth on her table.

But I had to be serious and very careful. In the war, I had had experience of mines. Here was one seated across from me.

'I'm not saying I'll make you as good a wife as Kate, but I'll do my best.' She dropped her voice and smiled lewdly. 'After we've eaten, we'll go upstairs. I want you to prove to me that making love should be done tenderly. Tulloch stabbed at me with that awful thing of his as if he wanted to hurt me. He did hurt me too. You won't, will you, Gregor?'

She had to be stopped, she had to be told that what she was saying was hysterical nonsense, but how to do it without hurting her feelings or causing her to scream, like a wounded ocelot?

'But, Millie,' I said, desperately and mendaciously, 'I promised Kate I would never marry again.'

'I'm surprised Kate made you give such a promise, but she wouldn't have if she'd known it was me you were going to marry. You see, when I visited her in hospital, just days before she died, we had a very private talk about you, Gregor. She said that she was worried about you. You pretended to be so sure of yourself, but you weren't really.'

Some of that was true, but what had it to do with Millie? Kate had liked her but hadn't respected her much, thinking her too submissive!

Thank heaven I would soon be safe in California.

'I was thinking of going with you to California, Gregor, but I was afraid it would spoil my chances of getting a quick divorce. So, I'm sorry, Gregor, I can't go with you.'

'That's all right, Millie. I understand.'

'Will you write to me?'

'Of course I will.'

'Every day?'

'I might not manage every day.'

'Well, twice a week at least. I'll write to you every day. I don't think I've got Madge's address.'

She ran out of the kitchen and in a minute was back with a writing pad and a pen.

I was tempted to write down a false address. A letter a day from Millie would rouse suspicions. Better if all those letters went astray.

But I could not bring myself to do it. I felt, obscurely, that I ought to be on Millie's side and not against her. So I wrote down the right address.

'Thanks, Gregor.' She flung her arms round my neck. Her lips kissed my ear. 'If we went upstairs, who would know?'

Who indeed? She didn't even have a cat.

The thought of doing away with her flitted into my mind. As she had said, who would know? Of course, it flitted out again just as fast.

Suddenly she let go of me and again ran out of the kitchen, in such a hurry that I thought she had an urgent need to go to the lavatory, having drunk too much wine and having eaten too much goulash.

She came louping in, as naked as an ocelot and as fierce-looking. I was reminded of a painting in the Glasgow Art Gallery, by a Dutch artist: the same doll-like face, small breasts, big stomach, sparse pubic hair, and knock-knees. One big difference, though, was that the woman in the painting looked wistful, whereas Millie looked rapacious.

With a twirl she turned round, showing me her most attractive feature. Alas, I saw only a pallid steatopygosity.

I felt pity, not desire. I realised that she was not right in her mind.

Had she really loved Tulloch and wanted him back, in spite of his cruelties?

'Take off *your* clothes, Gregor,' she whispered.

I had a memory, of childhood, myself aged five or so, and a girl – was her name Bessie Greenloaning? – also aged five, doing 'dirty things' in a coal cellar; that was, examining each other's private parts. Here I was, at 72, threatened with a similar experience.

'I want to see it, Gregor. Tulloch never let me see it. He made me hold it but he never let me see it.'

All I could say or rather stammer was 'I think you should go and put on your clothes, Millie.'

This was a woman whom for years I had looked on with lust but also with goodwill and affection. I owed her something, but how could I repay it? I remembered how she had ecstatically praised Tulloch to people who had known how contemptuously he had treated her. Still loving him, she was in a pitiful plight, from which there was no escape.

'Are you sure you don't want to go upstairs with me, Gregor?'

It was time for me to make my own escape. Excusing myself, I pushed past her and made for the hall. There I had some difficulty putting on my raincoat and hat, and getting my umbrella out of the stand. I was in a state of agitation.

She had not followed me into the hall. I could not see her but I heard her, weeping and wailing.

'Good night, Millie,' I cried, as I opened the outside door. 'Go to bed. You'll feel better in the morning.'

With that craven advice, I rushed out into the rain. I couldn't put up my umbrella, my hands had forgotten how to do it. I hardly knew where I was. I kept thinking that, if Millie was found dead in the morning, I would be to blame.

I thought of telephoning Morag McVey and asking her to go and see that Millie was all right but, if Millie wasn't all right, if she'd done away with herself, I would have involved myself.

The only person who could have helped Millie was a million miles away, in Mrs Cardross's arms.

Before I went to bed, I had decided to telephone Millie herself in the morning.

9

That Friday morning, I had promised myself to pay a visit to Kate's grave.

I kept hoping, and dreading, that Millie would telephone me but, by the time I was ready to go out, she hadn't, so, with some foreboding, I dialled her number. There was no answer. I let it ring for half a minute, but still there was no answer. Perhaps she was asleep.

I would try again when I came back from the kirkyard.

It was a cold dry morning. I did not take my car. The walk would do me good.

Grief should have had me stooped and shambling. My clothes should have shown signs of neglect, my shoes unpolished, the laces loose. Instead, I was as smartly turned out as ever. I walked briskly, with head held high. I lifted my hat, smiled, called cheerful greetings. It would be talked about in the tearooms.

They did not know, no one did, that from the age of eight, when my father had died, I had fought myself into the habit of never showing how unhappy I felt, how uncertain, how close to despair. I had kept it up all my life. It had won me my medal. It had earned me the reputation of being uncaring. That was how Hector saw me, and Chrissie, and my daughters, and Susan Cramond, and even, sometimes, my beloved Kate. I had loved Kate dearly but I had kept secrets from her and lied to her to protect my pose. But, after all those years, was it still a pose? Had I become what I outwardly appeared?

I was kenspeckle in the town, if not popular. Most people

knew that the red Mercedes, with the black upholstery belonged to me. It could be left parked in various places, night and day, without being vandalised. I might not have been liked but I was respected. I was asked to sing at concerts in aid of local charities and at Burns suppers. No golfer groaned when he saw on the notice-board that he had been drawn as my partner in a competition.

These were my reflections as I strode through the town and puffed up the brae to the kirkyard.

Tomorrow a new chapter in my life, perhaps the last chapter, would begin. Tomorrow fresh woods and pastures new. In California should I be a humble grateful old man, sunbathing on the patio, encouraging my grandchildren in their studies, reading worthy books, taking care not to upset my daughter and her husband, on Sundays accompanying them to their church, and, God forgive me, joining in their rollicking hymns?

Hat in hand, I stood by Kate's grave. Funeral wreaths, dusty and withered, still lay on it. There was as yet no headstone.

Or should I boldly enjoy myself? At the Country Club I had been a success on my last visit four years ago. Those good-hearted septuagenarians, every one a duffer at the game, had not been jealous of my prowess as a golfer. On the contrary, they had been proud of it. As for the ladies, especially the blue-haired elderly widows, they had been charmed by my manners and appearance. Kate had been amused, but she had been pleased too. I had flirted, but they had all seen that Kate was the one I loved. They had liked and admired her. 'Your good wife,' Mrs Birkenberger had said, for once not being sarcastic.

A robin came and perched on an adjacent headstone. It eyed me and then it defecated, daintily.

I heard Kate laughing. 'That's what it thinks of you, Gregor.'

I heard her weeping too. I was in tears myself.

I had already made not one but several Orphean journeys. I had not yet accepted her loss. I must, if I was not to go mad.

Would it be humbug for me to say that I ought to enjoy myself in California, not just for my own sake but for Kate's too, and for all those buried in the graves about me? Surely the dead must want the living to enjoy themselves, even those who had been curmudgeons when alive.

The robin flew off, with a chirp of goodwill.

I hadn't been home half an hour when the telephone rang. It was Helen Sneddon.

Her voice was sad. 'Were you out, Gregor? I phoned you half an hour ago.'

'Yes, I was out. I was paying a visit to Kate's grave.'

'Were you, Gregor?'

'Yes.'

'You won't have heard about Millie?'

My heart sank. 'No. What's happened?'

'She's been taken to Laudermuir.'

That was where deranged Lunderstonians were taken.

'Why? What's happened?'

'I'm not sure. I think she must have tried to harm herself.'

'Good God! Poor Millie.' Had she in her trauma mentioned me?

'According to Morag, the trouble is that she still wants Tulloch back.'

'Will she be all right? Eventually?'

'It seems she refuses to speak to anyone.'

'But they've got drugs that could help, haven't they?'

'Let's hope so.'

'You'll let me know how she gets on?'

'Yes, Gregor, I'll give you all the Lunderston news.'

'Thanks, Helen. Take care of yourself, and of Henry.'

'I doubt if he'll be here when you come back – if you come back. Goodbye, Gregor.' She put the telephone down.

It had, of course, occurred to me that I might never come back. I could die of a stroke in California. I could be killed in a car crash. I could be murdered. I could marry a rich old widow and end my days in a villa in La Jolla. Besides, what was there in parochial Lunderston to come back to? Kate's grave was there, but Kate as a memory would be with me wherever I was.

PART TWO

1

Wearing dark glasses, for San Diego's boast that it has the sunniest climate in the world is well justified, I came down the steps from the 747 smartly, as if after a flight of only an hour or so. Thanks to Susan Cramond in the first place and then to myself for having the poise and confidence to make full use of the first-class amenities, I had had a restful enjoyable journey and so had arrived fresh and bouncy. The stewardess who had looked after me, impressed by my patrician appearance and gracious manners, had taken me to be someone of importance, like an ambassador. So I was, but I was representing myself, Gregor McLeod. At the door of the plane she damned near curtsied. It was an auspicious beginning. In the game of brag that I was about to take part in, the players whom I would be trying to outwit and outface, one of whom I hoped would be Mrs Birkenberger, would have a lot more money than I but, to offset that, I had wit, style, a well-bred Edinburgh accent, and, above all, the ability to play golf well. With all that in my favour, I ought to do well.

Madge was waiting for me in the reception hall, looking so like her mother, tall and fair-haired, that I felt misgivings. If I was to win success here, I might have to do things that Kate would not have approved of.

Perhaps I had already done one.

Two elderly ladies had been about to engage a black porter and his luggage trolley when I had stepped in, looking and sounding as if my tip would be bigger than theirs. Naturally he had chosen me. The ladies had been disappointed, but not peevishly so. They had, after all, only one small suitcase between them, whereas I had two large ones and a bag of golf clubs.

We had parted amicably; indeed, they had wished me a nice day. Susan Cramond would have been proud of me, but would Kate?

'I see you've still got the knack,' said Madge, as we walked to the car followed by the porter. 'Frank never seems able to find a porter.'

I could have told her why. Frank's calculating eyes, behind the gold-rimmed spectacles, provoked other people into calculating too. Porters, adept at that kind of mental arithmetic, would see in a flash that his tip, adequate in his view, would be niggardly in theirs.

It was a small sign of my readiness for the campaign ahead of me that I had come with a supply of American money in units suitable for judicious tipping. I gave the man three dollars, which was too much but not ostentatiously so. I also thanked him in that sincere democratic way that Scots have but Americans do not.

I hadn't seen the car before: big, obese, black, and shiny, with many gadgets.

'It's Frank's,' said Madge. 'Mine is being repaired.'

'So he has got his vice-presidency at last?'

'No, he hasn't. He's hoping you can help him.'

'I?'

'Of course, it's ridiculous and you mustn't humour him.'

'Please explain.'

'You remember Mrs Birkenberger?'

'I remember her very well.'

'She's got a large account at Frank's bank. The man who's handling it at present is retiring soon. If Frank gets it he's sure to be made a vice-president. Millions of dollars are involved.'

We drove out of the car park.

'How does he think I can help?'

'She put in an appearance at the Country Club last week. Frank, against my wish I can assure you, went up to her and told her, as if she was the least bit interested, that you were coming for another visit.'

A shy man usually, Frank on the scent of money was as venturesome as a hyena.

'*Was* she interested?'

'She seemed to be. Anyway, she said you'd to be sure to give her a call. If it had been anyone else I'd have thought she was just being polite, but she's never that. He also told her that Mom had died.'

'Linda and I got on very well.'

'I didn't know you and she were on first-name terms.'

'Isn't everybody instantly on first name terms with everybody in America?'

'Did she actually call you Gregor?'

'She called me Professor.'

'But you were never a professor. Was she being sarcastic?'

'She expressed an interest in literature.'

'Don't be ridiculous, Dad. She's uneducated.'

'Not everybody has an honours degree in Economics, Madge. It didn't stop her from becoming a millionaire.'

'Her films were all rubbish.'

'Fascinating rubbish.'

'They made a lot of money, but I've heard you say that today people with paltry talents make fortunes.'

'True, but her talents were not paltry. Also, she was beautiful.'

'Her films have become a cult here. They still make money.'

'Good for Linda.'

Madge gave me a grim look. 'I don't know if you're really different now, Dad, or if, now that Mom's gone, I'm seeing you differently, but you strike me as being more, well, more above yourself, if you see what I mean. They thought you had class when you were here last time, they'll think it more now.

Looking at you, no one would guess you've just come ten thousand miles on a crowded plane.'

'Not so crowded in first class.'

'You didn't travel first class?'

'I did.'

'Good heavens!'

We were then driving along a ten-lane freeway. On either side the landscape was bright and arid. I remembered the misty greenness of home. But it was much too soon to be feeling nostalgic.

'California isn't the only place with munificent widows,' I said. 'Susan Cramond, whom you may remember at your mother's funeral, made up the difference between economy class and first class.'

'Was she the dour-faced old woman in the mink coat?'

'That was Susan.'

'I didn't know you and she were as friendly as that.'

'Susan has proposed that, when I return, she and I should go off together on a world cruise.'

'You're joking!' Her voice became stern. 'Were you and she carrying on while Mom was alive?'

'While your mother was alive, Madge, I wanted no one else.'

'This Mrs Cramond, is she well-off?'

'You saw her house. Her husband's family owned a steel-works.'

'You said she was a widow.'

'Yes.'

'Any children?'

'Three. All married. Eight grandchildren. One great-grand-child.'

'Would they like it if she married again?'

'She wouldn't give a damn whether they liked it or not. But who said anything about marriage? She's a formidable old lady and formidable old ladies make formidable wives.'

Madge gave a sob. 'It's not fair to Mom's memory, you being flippant like that.'

'I'm trying to be cheerful. Your mother would have wanted me to be cheerful, don't you think?'

She was silent. When she spoke again, she had changed the subject.

'I ought to warn you, Dad, Frank and I take our religion seriously.'

I could easily believe it in Frank's case, but not in hers. She had used to come home from Sunday school doubtful about what she had been taught. She was my daughter, after all.

'We don't allow alcohol in the house.'

'Oh.'

'Or smoking.'

'Not even cigars?'

'We had the house exorcised by Billy Malpass.'

'Billy Malpass, the spiritual plumber!' I cried.

'Don't mock, Dad. He came to our church to preach. He always offers to exorcise the houses of chosen elders.'

'And Frank came into that category? What form did this exorcising take?'

'He got rid of all alcoholic liquor.'

'By drinking it, do you mean?'

'No, I don't. By pouring it down the sink.'

In my bag I had a bottle of duty-free Glenmorangie. I was damned if I was going to pour it down the sink.

'What next?' I asked.

'He said a prayer in every room.'

'Including the john?' I could have added 'And the bedroom.'

'Please show respect, Dad.'

'What does the younger generation, Frank Junior and Midge, think of this?'

'They don't understand.'

In other words, they preferred to remain heathens.

'Does Malpass expect payment for these exorcisms?'

She hesitated. I knew her well enough to tell that the avarice of the man of God troubled her.

'He accepts a small honorarium. For charity. Not for himself.'

'How much?'

She shock her head. 'He gives spiritual comfort to millions.'

He didn't seem to have given her much, but I let it pass.

'Tell me about my grandchildren,' I said.

Midge's real name was Margaret but she had discarded it. She had not been pleased when I had told her that a midge in Scotland was a tiny insect with an itchy bite, that there were multitudes of them and they made people's lives a misery. That had been four years ago when she had been 15. Frank Junior, two years older, had struck me as typically American, amiable and naive. They were now students at the University of Southern California.

'They're all right,' said Madge, but because the Lord was listening, she had to tell the truth. 'They're not really all right. They're far from being all right. They're never at home. They prefer to live in squats with other students. It's all sex and drugs.'

'They'll grow out of it,' I said.

'That's what Frank says. You know how childishly hopeful he is.'

But why shouldn't he be hopeful when he was convinced the Lord was looking after him? A few small upsets would be put in his way, such as a son who took drugs, a daughter who was promiscuous, a wife who nagged, and a father-in-law who drank whisky on the sly, but in the end, lo, nirvana would be attained, in the shape of a vice-presidency and a bigger house with a bigger swimming pool.

2

In front of the house, an old rusty mustard-coloured banger was parked, plastered with stickers: there were at least 20. FUCKING IS FUN, proclaimed one. HAVE A SHITTY DAY, said another.

Loud music came from behind the house, where the pool was.

I felt indignant. They had no right to humiliate their mother in this way. I would have to talk to them.

Madge and I went in by the front door.

She showed me the room I was to use. Four years ago, I shared it with Kate. There had been a double bed then.

On a table by the bed was a Bible.

'We read from the Holy Scriptures every evening for half an hour, Dad. You're welcome to join us.'

Why not? There were many beautiful passages in the Bible.

'I'll get the children to bring in your suitcases and golf clubs.'

'Thank you, Madge.'

'Is it all right if the clubs go into the rumpus room?'

'That will do fine. I'll be taking them to the Country Club. I'll get a locker there.'

Madge went off and soon I heard her shouting instructions. I also heard Frank Junior. 'Has the old dude arrived?' Cheeky young bugger, thought the old dude.

Minutes later, Frank Junior came in burdened with my suitcases. Midge followed him. She said she had dumped the golf clubs in the rumpus room.

Both were chewing gum. Both stared at me guardedly.

Madge took herself off. I jaloused that she was giving me an opportunity to talk to my grandchildren.

'Sorry about Grandma,' said Frank Junior.

'She was a sweet old lady,' said Midge.

Both stopped chewing for a few seconds.

'We would have gone to the airport,' said Midge, 'but what would have been the point?'

'What indeed?'

'We would just have been in the way. But you made it all right.'

'Yes, thanks to your mother, I made it.'

'Did Mom tell you booze is out?' said Frank Junior with a grin.

'She did impart those dire tidings.'

'The bad news, eh? And no smoking. And no watching TV. You've come to Misery Hall, Grandad.'

'They've got religion,' said Midge, contemptuously.

If it was Aids they had, she'd have been more sympathetic.

'Did Mom tell you they had Billy Malpass driving out all impure spirits?' said Frank Junior.

'Yes, she mentioned it.'

'For five hundred dollars!'

'She didn't tell me that.'

'Malpass must be the biggest creep on earth,' said Midge.

He would have got my vote.

I had to speak up on behalf of my daughter.

'Don't you think you could show your mother more sympathy?'

'What's she got against pot?' asked Frank Junior. 'It's harmless.'

'And what's wrong with sex?' asked Midge. 'Sex liberates.'

I thought of Millie Tulloch locked up in the madhouse.

'Those stickers on your car,' I said. 'Couldn't you get rid of some of them? Your mother finds them humiliating.'

Madge came in then to ask me if I wanted anything to eat.

'No, Madge, not now. Frank Junior and Madge are just going out to get rid of some of those stickers on their car.'

Madge was surprised but pleased and grateful.

They looked at me balefully.

'Hot water and a scraper should do it,' I said.

They went out, chewing like mad.

'How did you manage it, Dad?' asked Madge.

'I don't know that I have, Madge.'

But when we looked out of the window, there they were, busy with hot water and scrapers.

Later, with the air conditioner making its racket, I lay on the bed, defiantly smoking a cigar, and wondering if I should return home early and take Susan at her word.

I must have dozed. Madge was knocking at the door. 'I'm going to fetch Frank, Dad. Would you like to come?'

'If you don't mind, I'd rather rest.'

'All right. The children have gone. If you're thirsty, there's plenty of Dr Pepper in the fridge. Won't be long.'

I awoke to see Frank gazing down at me.

'How are you, Dad?'

'Fine, thank you, Frank. How are you yourself?'

'Very well, thanks to the good Lord. Did you have a good flight?'

'An excellent flight, thank you, Frank.'

A note of awe came into his voice. 'Madge tells me you travelled first class.'

3

At the Country Club golf was a religion, anyone skilful was looked on as anointed, worthy of every honour and privilege. Few of the members rose to the level of mere competence. Four years ago, I had astonished them by going round their course with scores of under 80, which, for a man of my age, had struck them as miraculous. Nor was that all. Sometimes it happens that a player will return a score on paper which in reality out on the course had been a succession of lucky bounces and flukes, crudely executed. In my case this was not so. During my first round word had reached the clubhouse that the tall white-haired Scotsman was not only scoring brilliantly, he was also swinging beautifully. Members had tottered out onto the terrace to watch me play the difficult last hole. Inveterate hackers themselves, they were nonetheless theoretic experts, able to recognise and appreciate the skill that, with apparently minimum effort, achieves splendid results. Was it any wonder, they asked one another, as they watched me take four where they themselves usually took seven or eight, that the game had originated in St Andrews, Scotland?

During the three holes I had played with Mrs Birkenberger, she had asked me, after a particularly successful shot, if I was as good in bed. Though taken aback, I had replied that it wasn't for me to say, but the lady in bed with me. She had yelled with laughter and prodded me in the crotch with the club in her hand, a six-iron.

In the clubhouse afterwards, she had asked me, seriously it

71

seemed, to recommend a novel in which the characters had class. I had recklessly proposed *Middlemarch*, that grand but ponderous masterpiece, and I had reminded her that one of her best performances had been in a film adapted from George Eliot's *The Mill on the Floss*. She had played the part of Maggie.

She had been pleased. Few people, she had said, remembered that movie. It had been a box-office flop but an artistic success. She said she would read *Middlemarch*. Whether she had or not I never found out, for shortly afterwards she had gone off to her villa in Acapulco.

Madge had a part-time job with a firm of tax consultants but, four days after my arrival, she was free to drive me to the Country Club for my first game of golf. On the way, she lectured me. I had been accepted as a temporary member because I was good at golf, but also because I wasn't a Jew or a Chicano or a black or a loud-mouthed radical. People like those were taboo. She also warned me again about Mrs Birkenberger.

'Don't be seen being friendly with her, Dad.'

'Why not?'

'Because a lot of the lady members detest her. They think she's disgusting.'

'In what way disgusting?'

'I'd rather not say.'

'I never found her disgusting. A bit vulgar maybe, but not disgusting.'

'They say she hires young men.'

'To partner her at tennis?'

'Yes, but more than that.'

'Don't insinuate, Madge. Tell me frankly.'

'Well, they say she hires them to go to bed with her.'

'How do they know? Have they got spies in her household?'

'I don't know.'

'It's just a rumour then? A malicious rumour.'

'Anyway, I think you should avoid her.'

72

'What if she does not avoid me? You see, Madge, when I was here before, she asked me to recommend a novel. I suggested *Middlemarch*. She said she would read it.'

Madge laughed scornfully. *Middlemarch*? For goodness' sake, Dad. She wouldn't get past the first chapter.'

'But if she should want to discuss it with me, surely I should?'

'But not at the Club.'

'Perhaps not at the Club.' Few members of which, I was sure, had ever heard of *Middlemarch*.

'Where then?'

'At her house, perhaps?'

'She never invites anyone there.'

We arrived at the Club. As I got my golf clubs out of the boot, I was recognised and cordially greeted by members.

'Give me a call when you're ready to come home,' said Madge.

'Thank you, Madge.'

'Will you be all right, Dad? Her voice faltered. There were tears in her eyes.

'Yes, I'll be all right.'

But both of us knew that we would never be quite all right again, now that Kate was dead.

At that time of day, in the middle of the week, the members present were mostly as old as myself or older. Those who had already played their daily three or four holes rested in the lounge, virtuously exhausted, enjoying their beer and recalling, with harmless exaggerations, shots they had played, while others, who had still to go out to play, were blissful with anticipation.

It is not necessary to play golf well to enjoy it. Indeed, it could be argued that the duffer has a happier time hacking his way round for a score of 110 or so than the expert who moans over every shot lost to par and grumbles that his score of 78 would have been 75 but for some bad luck.

I gladly accepted the offer of a septuagenarian threesome to join them and make it a foursome. I laughed away their scruples that, not being in my class as a golfer, they might spoil my game and also that, not being as fit as I, they would not be able to play more than nine holes.

There was one aspect of golf at the Country Club that I did not like. This was the rule that electric carts had to be used. A rule for the benefit of slowcoaches prone to heart attacks was, I thought, a nonsense. They should have been persuaded to take up dominoes. I was, however, too diplomatic to say so.

My playing companions were Bud Hickson, owner of one of the biggest trucking firms in the State, Chuck Slocum, a retired big wheel in the Teamsters' Union, and, surprisingly, Hal Edison, ex-president of a bank: he was much more dignified in appearance and speech than his two cronies. All three were golf addicts. It would have been hyperbolical to say that they would have exchanged their large fortunes for my skill as a golfer, but they would have been tempted. To smite the ball a manly distance straight down the fairway would have given them more pleasure than possession of a new Rolls. A car, however opulent, was just a machine. A good golf swing was a gift from a greater god.

I shared a cart with Bud, who wore a white cap with St Andrews on the skip (he had once made a pilgrimage to the Old Course), a floral shirt, and tartan Bermuda shorts. He had a big heavy face, which indicated, wrongly, a surly nature. It also indicated, rightly, that he might be given to earthy speech.

Hal and Chuck, in the other cart, reminded me of Don Quixote and Sancho Panza, the former being tall, bony, and remote, and the latter short, stout, and hearty. Which of them, asked Bud, would I say had been in trouble with the law a few weeks back? The cops had raided a massage parlour downtown, looking for drug-pushers, they had claimed, but just for the hell of it, in Bud's view. Who did I think had been caught on the job with a fat Mexican whore? No, not Chuck. Old Hal, 'who looks more like a professor than you do, Gregor. It should have been hushed up. Hal's got friends in high places. But a journalist bastard got hold of the story and published it, with a picture. Hal's still in the doghouse with his wife Martha. Some dames in the Club wanted him thrown out, but Linda wouldn't have it. You remember Linda? Mrs Birkenberger. You played with her once. Used to be a famous film star. Past it now, but still one hell of a woman. By the way, not this Sunday but next, there's the Birkenberger Cup tournament for the over seventies. In memory of her first husband Al. Put your name down, Gregor. You'd win it by a mile.'

'Am I eligible?'

'Why the hell not? You're a member, ain't you?'

'Temporary.'

'With all rights and privileges. Get your name down, buddy. The winner gets invited to dinner at Linda's place, with his wife if he's got one. If he hasn't and Linda likes the look of him, he gets to go to bed with her. So they say, anyway. She liked the looks of you, Gregor, by all accounts.'

'Is your name down, Bud?'

'Sure is. So are Chuck's and Hal's. For the fun of it. None of us with a hope in hell, but I'd put money on you.'

Meanwhile, the game was proceeding. It had always amused me that men like Bud, Chuck, and Hal, who had spent a lot of time and money on tuition, had read books on the techniques of the game, and knew as well as any professional what was to be done and what was not to be done, nevertheless, when they had a club in their hands and a ball at their feet, forgot everything they had learned and swiped out with the same old frenzied speed. It was as if a civilised man reverted to Neanderthal habits in an instant. Bud in action was like a demented baboon, Hal like Quixote rushing at windmills, and Chuck like Sancho beating his donkey.

So wayward was their hitting that the two carts had to keep

zig-zagging across the fairways, like Dodgems at a fair. My own ball was usually where it was supposed to be, on the fairway. I was content to wait as my companions climbed stiffly out of their vehicles, swiped their balls to other unlikely and inconvenient spots, climbed in again, and made off in pursuit. I did not mind. The day was warm and sunny. The sky was blue. Unfamiliar birds sang unfamiliar songs. The course was beautiful with many clusters of poinsettias and other flowering bushes.

We played only eight holes and then sped towards the club-house. They led me straight to the notice-board and supervised my putting down my name on the list of entrants for Linda's cup.

Over ice-cold beers, Bud and Chuck advised me bawdily on how best to exploit my victory. A man capable of par at the par-three seventh, where the green was surrounded by water and where they themselves had taken eight and ten respectively, ought to be smart enough to get the better of Linda in bed, even if, as was rumoured, she made love like a hungry she-bear.

Hal did not join in the laughter. Having once been in charge of millions of dollars, he never saw anything to laugh at, not even in his having been caught in an adulterous act with a fat whore. Solemnly he assured me that, in his opinion, what Mrs Birken-berger needed was a man like me, tactful, educated, and courteous. The lady, he maintained, was desirous of improving her mind.

We were interrupted by a servant who said there was a telephone call for Mr McLeod.

'Excuse me, gentlemen,' I said, rising. 'It'll be my daughter.'

'No, sir,' said the servant, as we walked away. 'It's Mrs Birkenberger.'

4

My hand shook, my heart thumped, my mouth was dry, as I picked up the telephone. This could be the beginning of an adventure as wondrous as any of Ulysses'.

'Gregor McLeod speaking,' I said, as suavely as I could.

'Hello, Professor. It's a pleasure to hear you again.'

Her voice was not euphonious, but neither was it aggressive.

'I called your daughter and she told me you were at the Club.'

So poor Madge was hoping after all that I might be able to help Frank get that account.

'Your son-in-law, the goofy guy that works in the bank, called me yesterday to say that you were back in San Diego.'

'He shouldn't have bothered you, Linda. You don't mind my calling you Linda?'

She laughed. 'You have my permission, Professor.' She became serious. 'I was sorry to hear about your wife. I remember her well. A tall white-haired lady with an honest smile and a voice I could have listened to all day.'

Yes, that was Kate. But perhaps 'honest', though very appropriate, was rather a strange word to use. Could there possibly be an insinuation that my smiles were not so honest?

'I had a chat with her once, you know.'

I hadn't known. Kate had never mentioned it.

'I know how you must feel, Professor.'

Had she lost someone whom she had loved? I tried to remember if any of her husbands had died while she was married to him. Yes, her first, old Al Birkenberger.

'My sister Margarita died when she was ten. I was eight.'

That must have been over 60 years ago. Linda had kept her childhood a secret. As I had myself.

'Would you believe I still miss her? Most people don't know I had a sister. I would have told your wife about her. So, since she isn't here, I've told you.'

'I feel honoured, Linda.'

Her tone changed. 'Do you remember, Professor, you recommended a book to me? *Middlemarch* by George Eliot.'

It had been like sending a novice climber up the north face of the Eiger.

'Yes, I remember. I'm sorry if you found it hard going.'

'I didn't ask for something easy. I asked for something with class. I guess it's got plenty of that. I've read it three times.'

But how much of it had she understood?

'I often read bits of it. Like some people read the Bible. It's boring as hell in places but I've stuck with it. I reckon it must have real class if it bores me and yet makes me want to go on reading it.'

'It is that kind of book.'

'I'd like to discuss it with you, Professor.'

'Any time, Linda.'

'Why not now? There's a car on its way to pick you up. That's if you don't mind having lunch with an old woman as common as shit.'

I managed not to gasp at the deliberate vulgarity. Was she testing me in some way? Or was she showing her opinion of the very proper heroines of *Middlemarch*, Dorothea and Rosamund?

Trying to hide my excitement I went back to my friends.

'Well, was it your daughter?' asked Bud.

'No. It was Mrs Birkenberger.'

Bud and Chuck laughed.

'Are you sure it wasn't Nancy Reagan?' said Bud.

'She's invited me to lunch. There's a car coming for me.'

'Good God, the guy means it,' cried Bud.

He and Chuck looked concerned.

'What's she up to?' asked Bud. 'You're a swell guy, Gregor, and you've got a beautiful golf swing, but you're no match for Linda. She'll chew you to pieces.'

'She's done it before. The poor guys were never the same again,' said Chuck.

'The lady does not take kindly to fortune-hunters,' said Hal. 'But Gregor is different.'

Well, how different was Gregor?

The servant came then to say the car had arrived.

Off I went, smiling. I made for the gents', not only to empty my bladder but also to comb my hair and smooth my moustache. Looking at my face in the mirror, I tried not to see a fortune-hunter.

The car was a white Cadillac. The door was being held open for me by a Mexican chauffeur.

What, I wondered, as I lay back on the luxurious cushions, would the Druids of Murchison's tearoom have said if they had seen me then?

I let myself dream. Linda and I fell in love. We got married. Stranger things had happened, especially in California. It wouldn't last long but, during it, the magic of great wealth would be mine. That villa in Acapulco. De luxe hotels all over the world. Golf with famous professionals.

These, though, were a fortune-hunter's ambitions. I rejected them. My purpose was to help the lady improve her mind. Without offending her – it would take great tact – I would persuade her that expressions like 'as common as shit' were unworthy of her.

The chauffeur turned and smiled. 'I am Miguel, sir,' he said.

'How do you do, Miguel? My name is Mr McLeod.'

'English, sir?'

'No. Scottish.'

'Is it not the same?'

'No. There are many differences.'

For instance, the Scots were the most democratic, the most approachable, of people. They had the knack of being friendly without subservience or sycophancy.

5

It was a half-hour's ride, through semi-desert. The house could be seen far off, a white flash on a green hill. According to Frank, Mrs Birkenberger had bought it for $ 3,000,000 after the death of the man who had had it built. He had been a recluse, which explained its isolation, its 12-foot fence, its iron gates, and its armed guards. These last were now demanded by the insurance company because of the paintings that Mrs Birkenberger perversely kept in the house instead of hiding them away in a bank vault.

The misanthrope must have loved birds, bees, and butterflies, for he had planted for their delight all round the house and on the slopes of the hill a vast garden of flowers, fragrant shrubs, and trees with blossoms. Scattered about were statues dressed only in moss and lichens. He had not minded talking to people as long as they were made of marble or bronze.

The house itself, two-storeyed, was white with red shutters. Bougainvillea climbed to the upper windows. There was a spacious terrace with many pots and urns bright with flowers.

As I got out of the car and breathed in the perfumed air I felt I had outdone Ulysses. In his travels, he had never reached Elysium.

Down the steps from the terrace came not my hostess, but a different woman altogether. About 40, tall, black-haired, grave-faced, and wearing a plain dark blue dress with no jewellery, not even rings, she was, I could not help thinking, more suited to be mistress of this splendid estate. When she spoke, I was not surprised to find her voice deep, but quiet and pleasant.

'Good afternoon, Mr McLeod,' she said, smiling. 'I'm Sarah Morland, Mrs Birkenberger's housekeeper. She would like you to join her on the patio.'

She led me through large sunny rooms to French windows that gave onto a patio shaded by a large magnolia tree. There sat Linda, wearing dark glasses and holding a book. Just below was a swimming pool four times the size of Frank's, and in the distance, blue also but hazier, shone the immeasurable Pacific.

In her daffodil-yellow blouse and pants of pillarbox red, Linda hardly looked a likely owner of this Elysian domain. Yet she was curiously beautiful. Her face was smooth and her neck, also 70 years old, was plump when it ought to have been scraggy. Disconcerting too was the blackness of her hair, with not a single white or grey one to be seen. But what made her an improbable châtelaine was her voice. Though an accomplished actress, able to imitate any accent, even that of Dorothea Brooke in *Middlemarch*, she spoke as she must have done many years ago when a waitress in a greasy spoon. Had it to do with some misguided conception of honesty?

'Hi, Professor,' she said, taking off her glasses. 'Take a seat. You'll be tired after the golf.'

'Linda, this is an enchanting place.'

She laughed. 'What am I then? The princess to be rescued from the ogress, or the ogress herself?'

Her eyes, violet in colour, were far from meek. Her wide lively mouth would never be prim.

Years ago, on a conducted tour of the Palais Real in Madrid, with its 2800 rooms (only 45 were on view) and its inexhaustible display of beautiful artefacts, chandeliers, tapestries, paintings, clocks, porcelain, silverwork, and furniture, the guide had pointed to the portrait of the king whose idea it had been to build and furnish that magnificent palace: a small insignificant señor who wouldn't have been noticed in any Spanish street. I had wondered if possession of great wealth and the magnificence it could bring about inevitably bestowed a distinction on the owner.

Did Linda show any signs of such a distinction? It seemed to me she did, though I would have found it hard to describe.

'Would you like something to drink, Professor?' she asked.

'Thank you, Linda. Some white wine, perhaps?'

She did not ring a bell, she bawled.

'You're looking very well, Professor,' she said.

'May I return the compliment?'

'How long are you going to be in California?'

'I haven't decided yet. No great hurry, mind you, to return to Scotland in the winter.'

'I've never been to Scotland. I hear it's a beautiful country.'

A manservant appeared, Chinese, in white jacket and black trousers.

'Chung, a bottle of our best white wine, chilled.'

'Yes, madam.'

'And tell them in the kitchen we'll eat out here, in twenty minutes. That suit you, Professor?'

'Admirably.'

'You can take off your coat if you like.'

'Thank you.' I removed my black blazer with the Lunderston Golf Club crest in gold and placed it over the back of my chair.

'I see you've been tackling *Middlemarch* again,' I said.

'I've got a question to ask you, Professor. Is there any sex in it?'

I blinked. 'Theses have been written on that theme.'

'I guess so, but what's your opinion?'

'I think there's sex all right but, of course, it's suppressed. In those days women of the upper class were not supposed to have sexual feelings.'

'I bet they masturbated like mad.'

I blinked again.

'Dorothea's all mind and no body,' said Linda. 'See that statue?'

It was a nymph beside the pool, coyly pressing her thighs together; not that there was anything to hide.

'All shut up,' said Linda. 'No way in. Not ever. That's how I see Dorothea.'

Chung appeared with the wine in a bucket of ice, and two glasses.

Linda waited till he was gone.

'Do you know how old Dorothea is?' she asked.

'I know she's very young.'

'She's nineteen. At nineteen, Professor, girls are as hot-assed as boys. Today, then, a thousand years ago.'

I not only blinked then, I gawked, at the idea of Dorothea being hot-assed.

'You'll have heard of Billy Malpass, Professor? Famous evangelist.'

Famous exorciser. 'Yes, Linda, I've heard of him.'

'I once sat beside him at a big dinner in Washington. The President was present. I told him, Malpass, I mean, that it couldn't have been Samson's hair that his wife cut off. How could that have taken away his strength? No, it must have been his balls.'

'And what did Mr Malpass say?'

'Give him his due, he said it was an interesting theory. But then he was after a big donation.'

'Did he get it?'

'No, he didn't.'

Two little maids then appeared, both dark-skinned, and began to prepare the table for lunch. Their mistress spoke to them in Spanish. They answered respectfully but freely. They were at ease in her presence.

I wasn't, not yet, not altogether.

To make conversation, I said that the housekeeper, Ms Morland, seemed remarkably well-bred.

'So she is. Grandfather was a US Senator. Her father's a famous surgeon.'

84

Why then was she here as a servant? I did not ask it aloud.

'She's a very attractive woman,' said Linda.

'Very.'

Linda smiled. 'Are you thinking of making a pass at her, Professor? You wouldn't be the first.'

'But, Linda, I'm a guest in your house.'

'Shit, guests in my house have made passes at me.'

'That, if I may say so, is not quite the same thing.'

'So you think it would be all right for you to make a pass at me but not at Sarah?'

'What I meant was that the relationship of guest to hostess is one that might, without impropriety, ripen into something deeper and more intimate.'

She laughed. 'Now you're talking like a character in *Middlemarch*. They wrap up what they say in a lot of big words because they're afraid of telling the truth about themselves and one another.'

She must have read that in a book.

'By the way, Professor,' she said, with a change of tone, 'I'd like you to know that Sarah's not just my housekeeper. She's my friend. Let me tell you about her, before someone else does. When she was twenty, about seventeen years ago, she shot a man, killed him.'

I was shocked but not surprised. Such a doom was written on Morland's tragic face.

'The bastard had raped her young sister. So Sarah shot him. I'd have shot him too but first I'd have cut his balls off. He was highly connected, so Sarah got seven years in prison. She should have got a medal. Her sister drowned herself.'

The food then arrived. It was delicious and plentiful: crabmeat salad, smoked salmon, the tenderest of roast beef, the freshest of strawberries, and new-baked bread. The wine, red and white, was vintage French.

I would have enjoyed it a lot more if I hadn't kept thinking about Morland. It wasn't only pity for her that troubled me, it was also that my sucking up to Linda had been revealed as insincere and self-seeking.

'To get back to *Middlemarch*,' said Linda, 'was Mr Casaubon a queer, but George Eliot didn't know it? That happens in books. So Josh Bolton told me. You'll have heard of Josh?'

I nodded. Bolton had written a novel about his war experiences, so bloody, obscene, and scatological that it had made him world-famous and earned him a fortune, which he had squandered on expensive wives.

'Josh told me that often writers don't understand the characters in their own books. Hell, why should they? Half the time we don't understand ourselves.'

'Perhaps we don't try hard enough,' I said. 'Perhaps we're afraid of what we might find out.'

'No perhaps about it. Tell me about Scotland. Do you wear a skirt there?'

'You mean a kilt? Yes, I've worn a kilt. I have a Highland name.'

As a matter of fact, I always wore one at golf-club functions and Burns suppers.

Linda suddenly stood up. She had eaten and drunk very little. 'You'll excuse me, Professor, if I leave you. Time for my siesta. Finish your lunch. Stay as long as you like. If you'd like to look round, Sarah will show you.'

'I'd like to see your paintings, Linda. I believe you've got a Rembrandt self-portrait.'

'Sure. I'll let Sarah know. I have a car I seldom use, Professor. If you want, you can have the use of it.'

'Thank you very much, Linda. It will be very useful.'

I almost said that it would enable me to visit her often but I stopped myself in time.

She went off into the house.

It was stupid of me, there was no justification whatever

for it, but I felt that a bond of trust had been established between us.

I drank more wine than I should, considering that I was going to drive myself home in the loaned car.

Ms Morland came to take me to see the paintings.

I had decided to behave towards her as if I did not know her story. That way, she would not become a complication.

The room where the paintings were kept had a steel door disguised as wood. Inside Ms Morland pressed a button. Steel shutters slid back. Light poured in, and there was old Rembrandt Van Rijn in his nightcap, with boozy nose, raddled cheeks, and ironic eyes.

On a pedestal was the bronze bust of an old man, gaunt and wrinkled.

'Mr Birkenberger,' said Ms Morland. 'He bought all these paintings. At that time they could be had relatively cheaply. If you knew what to buy. It appears he did.'

'My son-in-law says they're worth twenty million.'

'A lot more than that.'

'Does Mrs Birkenberger come here often?'

'Yes. She's very proud of them.'

'So she should be. They're marvellous.'

I went from painting to painting, from Cézanne to Van Gogh, from Matisse to Lautrec.

There were nudes. I found myself wondering what Ms Morland would look like with her clothes off.

I was immediately rebuked by Rembrandt's ironic wink.

Ms Morland must have been impressed by the seriousness with which I was studying the paintings.

'If you would like to stay for a while, Mr McLeod—'

'No, no. I'll go. I hope to be back often.'

She escorted me to the terrace. At the foot of the steps was a small red Buick.

6

Like the predestinarians of 17th-century Scotland, Frank believed that the Lord had favourites who could do no wrong. In his case they were the rich. If they were also white Americans, they were twice blessed. Mrs Birkenberger was not quite in the top echelon of these elect, not because of her numerous marriages, which were covered by her certificate of exemption, but because she was part Mexican and suspected to have Catholic origins. Nonetheless, by making her *very* wealthy, the Lord had shown He did not hold those blemishes against her. Therefore, none of His adherents should.

When he heard that I had had lunch with her, he was ecstatic and, when he saw the car she had lent me, he could not have been more awed if it had been made of gold.

'You must really have impressed her, Dad.'

'I don't know about that, Frank, but she certainly impressed me. She's a fascinating woman.'

'Did she mention me at all?'

I could hardly say that she'd called him the goofy guy that worked in the bank.

'She mentioned that you'd let her know I had come.'

Madge was listening to this with a face of misery. The reason had nothing to do with me and my relationship with Mrs Birkenberger. It had to do with Midge.

That young lady had telephoned to tell her mother that she was pregnant, and the student responsible was black.

I was sceptical. 'She didn't look pregnant the last time I saw her,' I said.

'But, Dad, why would she tell me such a monstrous lie?'

'Well, Madge, I think she's putting you and Frank to a test. You say you've given yourself to Jesus, so you ought to be able to welcome with love any unfortunate grandchild Midge presented you with. By making it black she's made the test all the harder, that's all.'

'It would be your great-grandchild, Dad,' said Madge. 'If it was black, would you cherish it?'

'I've not been born again, Madge. I've not given myself to Jesus.'

Therefore, I was still at liberty to allow myself all my human prejudices.

'But, Madge, I assure you there's no child, black or white, in the offing. It's a bluff.'

She considered. She dried her eyes. She nodded. 'Thanks, Dad. I think you're right. She's just testing me. You too, Frank.'

'Yes, honey, me too.' Frank's voice was sad. He knew he had failed the test. Jesus might punish him by not letting him have Mrs Birkenberger's account.

That might not depend on Jesus, Frank. It might depend on me.

'I'm surprised that she didn't ask if you'd approve of an abortion,' I said.

'She did,' said Madge.

'That surely settles it. She *was* testing you. I don't know Midge as well as I should but I know her well enough to be convinced that the last thing she wants, at this time in her life, is a child, particularly a black one.'

'Dad's right,' said Frank. 'Honey, we're worrying about nothing.'

I could have said, Frank, you should be worrying about the dubiousness of your love for Jesus. But I didn't say it. We were all hypocrites in our own way.

I excused myself and went to lie down in my room.

90

They must have thought I had fallen asleep, or else they forgot how thin the walls were. They discussed me, in whispers, but I heard most of it.

'Didn't you say,' said Frank, 'that he had an unhappy childhood?'

'Jean and I often thought he must have, but we didn't really know, he never talked about it, not even to Mom.'

'And he's never spoken about his parents?'

'I've never even seen a picture of them. I think his father died when he was a child. I just don't know about his mother.'

Then they must have realised that I might be listening, for either they dropped their voices or they went into another room.

7

At the Country Club the red Buick was at once recognised as belonging to Linda. It was taken as a sign that I had already begun to enjoy the lady's favours. Reactions varied. Some elderly widows were cross with me. Come-hither smiles turned to go-to-hell scowls. In the men's locker room, according to Bud, there was some ribald jesting at my expense, but it was good-natured and congratulatory. They paid me the compliment of assuming that I was in it for the money and, having in their day brought off lucrative business deals, risky and not altogether honest, they looked upon my pursuit of Linda as a similar venture and wished me well. The general opinion, however, was that, if I was after a widow with money, I would do better to make a bid for Mrs Harrington, who might not have Linda's immense wealth and fame but didn't have her temper either. A sweet-natured dim-witted old lady, she would not object to my playing golf as often as I wished. Also she would never notice if I had adventures on the side. Linda, on the other hand, might take it into her head to ban golf altogether and God help me if I as much as smiled at another woman.

I put up with all the chaffing like a good sport but took care not to join in any denigration of Linda. According to Chuck, there was a belief that she had spies at the Club.

While waiting for another invitation or summons, I took a notion to go downtown and drop into one of the run-down hotels that catered for penurious pensioners and have a chat with some of them. I would go by bus. That would be part of the exercise.

It would be salutary for me after my consorting with the smug pampered well-off members of the Club.

On Saturday morning I mentioned at breakfast that I was going downtown.

'If it's anything special you want, Dad,' said Madge, 'College Grove Shopping Center's a lot nearer.'

'No. I want to go downtown.'

'All right. We'll go with you. Won't we, Frank?'

'Sure will,' said Frank, ever willing to help one who had not yet helped him.

'If you don't mind, I'd rather go by myself.'

'Oh.'

Into that small word much suspicion was crammed. Downtown were porno movies, dirty-bookshops, massage parlours, and topless bars. Madge had had a letter from Jean. Probably my remark about the whorehouses of Tijuana had been quoted in it.

I had a little lie ready. 'I'd like to go to the Public Library and have a look at some British newspapers. The papers here never have any British news.'

'Are you feeling homesick, Dad?' asked Madge.

'Not particularly.'

'Are you sure you could drive yourself? You'd have to use the freeway.'

'I'm going by bus.'

'Bus?'

She and Frank looked at each other in amazement that quickly turned to horror.

'Why on earth should you go by bus, Dad? If you don't want to drive, either Frank or I will take you.'

'Sure will,' said Frank.

'What's wrong with going by bus?' I asked. 'I've travelled in buses at home.'

'It's different here, Dad. Only blacks and poor whites ride the buses. The one you'd have to use takes over an hour and goes through a black district. You'd feel very much out of place. Wouldn't he, Frank?'

'Sure would.'

'Out of place among my fellow human beings?'

'You know what we mean.' Madge's voice was sharp.

'I've never been on a city bus myself,' said Frank, 'but I guess it must be an uncomfortable experience. Dangerous, too. You could pick up some disease. Another thing, Dad, people on their own are often mugged in broad daylight downtown, only a few yards from the main street.'

Only a few yards, therefore, from the business area, where his and other banks rose 20 storeys high, the cathedrals of our age.

'You would be the only white person on the bus,' said Madge. 'You'd be surrounded by big fat black women and their screaming piccaninnies. You'd love that.'

In my room, getting ready, I studied myself in the mirror. Good bone structure. Wide brow. Firm but sensitive mouth. Commanding nose. Abundant white hair. All those were gifts of nature. Who would blame me for practising tilts of the head to achieve the full patrician effect? A champion of the poor and oppressed ought never to be sullen and hangdog. Had not Sir Galahad been the noblest knight, with the most costly caparison?

Making the joke, I heard the rustle in the undergrowth where lurked hideous memories that no shining sword could slay.

I had to walk a quarter of a mile to wait for a bus. In that district, where every household owned at least two cars, few people were ever seen waiting at bus-stops. I was alone, therefore. Since the morning was warm and sunny, I wore no jacket, only a white open-necked shirt and a pale blue cashmere pullover, the best that Hawick could produce. My tan slacks were Daks. Drivers of passing cars glanced at me in surprise. If any had stopped to offer me a lift, I was prepared to decline with a chuckle, letting it be deduced that I was not travelling by bus because I was poor, but for a subtler, more intriguing reason.

At last the bus came. As I stepped on board, the driver looked as if he was tempted to advise me to take a taxi. I slipped my nickel and quarter into the slot and then had a choice of 50 seats, for the bus was as yet empty.

In the black district, the houses were smaller, little better than shacks, the shops tawdry, the churches numerous but hardly inspiring. The bus-stops were thronged. A big fat black woman with a heavy shopping bag sat beside me and crushed me against the side. I smiled to show that I did not mind, but she ignored me. They all did. I might as well not have been there. They thought I was being patronising. If they could have afforded to go by car or taxi, they would have. Why didn't I? What was my game?

The superabundance of churches – I stopped counting at 35 – surely proved true Marx's dictum that religion was the opium of the masses. Every Sunday, black preachers would rant about the everlasting glory to come. Their congregations, drugged by that promise, accepted meekly their earthly misery.

In America, poverty was a culpable state. The poor were blamed, not pitied. To take help from public funds was as bad as stealing. In Britain too that had been the case 30 years ago. In my ILP days I had played a small part in making society a little more humane.

The bus put me down near Frank's bank, huge as an iceberg, glittering in the sun. I had visited him in it once. It had marble floors and pillars in the main hall, and yet it was only a few minutes' walk from the doss-houses where the winos and drop-outs lived. In his office, with the Stars and Stripes on his desk and a portrait of the President on the wall, Frank worked hard and conscientiously to make more money for his bank and therefore for himself. In his earnest way, he had explained that the more he earned, the more tax he would pay, thus doing his duty by the poor.

The Reading Room was upstairs. Madge had warned me that its frequenters would be out-of-work misfits, all men and all shabbily dressed. She was right. Most were elderly. Few had come to read. What was happening in the world or in their own country was no concern of theirs. No one cared whether they existed or not. They stood or sat staring at newspapers or magazines, occasionally they turned a page, but they took nothing in. There was an air of disuse or uselessness about them. In the richest country in the world, they had nothing to look forward to. They came here every day because, if they did not speak or eat or spit – notices forbade such practices – they would be tolerated. The room was bare and the chairs hard but it must have seemed palatial compared with the cubby-holes where they slept.

Another peculiarity of America, or at any rate of California, was that the old, or, to use the fashionable euphemism, senior citizens, liked to herd together. There were the dingy downtown hotels for those with no other means but their State pensions, and at the other end of the social scale the Ranchos, green oases on the outskirts of the city where retired people with money bought big houses and had every amenity laid on for them, including geriatric golf.

In a corner were racks of newspapers, some from American towns I had never heard of, such as Coos Bay, but there was no *Guardian* or *Telegraph* or *Times*.

To be fair, if an American went into the public library in some Scottish provincial town such as Dundee, looking for the *San Diego Tribune*, he wasn't likely to find it.

Frank had advised me to ask at the desk. This I did, politely.

My politeness wasn't appreciated. The woman in charge was middle-aged and grey-haired. She looked at me with what seemed disapproval. She thought that a man so well dressed and well-spoken could afford to buy any newspaper he wanted to read.

'We've only got the London *Times*,' she said, pushing a slip of paper across the counter. 'Write your name and address.'

I did so.

'How many d'you want?'

'Two or three of the latest issues, please.'

'Write three then.' She showed me where.

She took three copies of *The Times* from a shelf behind her.

'Thank you very much,' I said.

'You're welcome.'

I went over to a table at which only one man was sitting. Other tables had four or five at them.

I looked through the newspapers. There was very little news of Scotland.

There was an account of a debate in Parliament on the subject of devolution. My own view on home rule for Scotland was simple. All my life I had wanted Britain to be a socialist country. That I might have hated to live in it, as my daughters and the Druids of Murchison's tearoom had often taunted, was beside the point. Not that it would ever happen. The English would prevent it. Those lord-lovers would always give the Tories a majority. On its own, Scotland might have become socialist if it had not lost faith in itself. Tamely the Scots had let themselves be cheated out of nationhood.

Absorbed in these reflections, I was slow to notice the stink near me, rubbing elbows with me, in fact.

The man was as old as myself. There was nothing to be seen to account for the awful smell. It was not simply cloacal. His clothes were shabby but clean enough: they looked as if they had been supplied by the Salvation Army. His face was shrivelled, his hands bony and mottled. There were no visible suppurations, gangrenes, eczemas, or oozing boils.

The fact that its source was unknown somehow made it all the more horrible. It should also have made it more pitiable.

Another man came and sat at the table. After a few seconds, he muttered, 'Jesus Christ!' and got up and moved away.

Illness could humiliate. The poor fellow must know that he exuded this stench of decay, disease, and mortality. Where could he go that it would not offend anyone? There were many such places in California, with its enormous deserts, but perhaps he needed the company of people, even of people who could not bear his presence.

There were notices enjoining silence, but surely no committee framing rules and no woman appointed to see that they were observed would have objected to a whispered 'What is wrong, friend? Is there anything I can do to help?'

I did not say it. Instead I tried to read a witty article on the badness of food in British roadside restaurants.

Two men at the counter were talking to the attendant and looking in the direction of my companion. They were protesting about his presence.

I wished the unfortunate man would go of his own accord and spare everybody the unpleasantness of seeing him ordered out.

The attendant came over and stood beside us. Her nose twitched. In this land of gadgets, there was none to assess the amount of human stink allowable in a public library.

On her dour face appeared for a few seconds a gentleness of pity.

He got up and crept out of the room, with a shame and weariness poignant to behold.

'If I get complaints,' she said, 'I've got to act on them. Was he bothering you?'

She did not wait for an answer. It was as well, for it would have taken me a long time to find one.

Out on the street, I did not now have the impudence to venture into a pensioners' hotel with my dubious solicitude.

All of me shaky, especially my legs, I went into the first bar I came to. I almost ran out again for it had a jukebox blaring pop music and barmaids with bare bosoms, but I slunk over and crouched in a corner.

The girl who swaggered over to take my order was chewing gum. She had hard eyes, dyed-blonde hair, and big breasts, but she was young and healthy and smelled like roses. I could not resist sniffing gratefully.

How could I have explained to her that she represented not a means of stimulating enfeebled lust but the sweetness and good-ness of life itself? Alas, she misinterpreted my sniffing. No doubt in the hope of a tip made generous by guilt, she let her left breast touch my cheek as she bent down to wipe the table.

'Smell all you want, Grandpa,' she said.

I had meant to order beer for it was too early for whisky but I found myself whimpering, 'A scotch, please, with water.'

'You foreign? Where from? Let me guess. Poland?'

I shook my head.

'Ireland?'

This time I nodded. Let Ireland be given the discredit of the sniffing old lecher.

'It'll be Irish whiskey then?'

I nodded.

When she came back with the whiskey, I gave her a dollar as a tip. It was more than generous, but she seemed displeased. She thought I should have paid for the sniffs.

I took a taxi home, though it cost $20.

8

As soon as I got home, Madge, in a panic, insisted that all the clothes I was wearing must be immediately washed and fumigated. After that, they would be put in a black plastic bag and given to the Salvation Army. I demurred, for they had cost me a lot of money, I felt comfortable in them, and I thought she was exaggerating the fear of disease. Then I was ordered to use disinfectant soap when taking my shower. Heaven knew what germs I had picked up.

I didn't ask her – I was too ashamed – how I was to cleanse my mind of the memory of that unhappy man creeping off to a bitter loneliness, with no one to give him a pat on the shoulder or a word of comfort.

I knew what she would have answered. 'Just forget it, Dad. There's nothing you could have done, there's nothing you can do, to help. So just forget it.'

And she would have been speaking for the world. Certainly Frank concurred.

I did not tell them of my own agony in the topless bar.

In the afternoon, Frank Junior and Midge visited the house. They were in a forgiving tolerant mood. Midge forgave her mother for being so stupid as to believe the lie about the pregnancy and Frank Junior, who wanted money from his father, was unusually prepared to be broad-minded as to how his father earned it.

They were not interested in my story about the man in the library. 'Down-and-outs are ten a penny downtown.'

I felt sad. They were the young, in whose keeping should have been the ideals not only of their own country but of all humanity.

Frank Junior was studying philosophy. 'You know what Socrates said, Grandad. Know yourself. Well, man's a selfish acquisitive animal, isn't he? He still is, after thousands of years. So we can assume he always will be. So he shouldn't waste time thinking he can improve.'

Midge was a student of contemporary history. 'Didn't your Prime Minister say that, if the Good Samaritan hadn't made a lot of money, then he couldn't have done his good deed? Neither he could, could he?'

Seeing me in discussion with her children, Madge was grateful to me. 'I'm glad you're taking an interest in them, Dad. They have respect for you.'

They were very enthusiastic when they heard that I had had lunch with Linda.

'Gee, Grandad, that was great. You know, her films have become a cult.'

'Is her place as beautiful as they say?'

'Did you meet Morland? Lots of people would like to meet her.'

'Will you be going back, Grandad?'

'Could you get us invited? It would be fabulous if you could.'

'She's been married five times. Do you think she's got her eye on you for her sixth?'

All that could have been parried with a few witty rejoinders, if only they hadn't spoken with absolutely no humour. They were as serious as brain surgeons during an operation.

Later, I was resting in my room when I heard the telephone ring. Madge answered it. Soon she was knocking on my door. 'Dad, it's for you. Mrs Birkenberger.'

I got off the bed.

'Take it in Midge's room, Dad. It's more private.'

In Midge's room there were no chairs, just cushions on the floor. I sat cross-legged, like Buddha. Posters showing famous pop stars covered the walls. As I picked up the telephone, a memory of childhood came into my mind. A neighbour had given me a black tin box containing marbles; it had belonged to her son, who had recently died. Instead of the coloured clay marbles that I had expected and that I would have been happy to see, for I couldn't afford even those, cheap though they were, there before my eyes were dozens of beautiful glassies, as we called them, with whirls and whorls of brilliant colours. It was a treasure. Now my hands were shaking as they had been then, as if I was about to open another black box.

'Hello, Linda,' I said. 'How pleasant to hear from you again. I hope you're remembering you've to present the Cup tomorrow.'

'What cup?'

'The Birkenberger Cup. A tournament for the over-70s. Tomorrow. I'm thought to have a good chance of winning.'

She laughed. 'In that case, Professor, it will be an extra pleasure to present it. I'm afraid I had forgotten all about it. What I'm phoning for is to ask you and your daughter and her husband to come to dinner tonight.'

It *was* another black box, full of marvels. 'For myself, Linda, I'll be delighted to come.'

'Go and ask them.'

'Yes, of course, but I'm sure they'll be delighted too.'

'There will be only the four of us.'

I rushed into the sitting-room.

'She wants us to go to dinner tonight,' I cried.

'Us?' said Madge.

'Yes, you, Madge, Frank, and me.'

'At her house?'

'Yes.'

'Tonight?'

'Yes.'

'She's not giving us much notice, is she?'

'Never mind that, honey,' cried Frank. 'Go and tell the lady that we're honoured by the invitation.'

Madge said nothing, but looked sour.

I hurried back to the telephone. 'We're all delighted to accept, Linda.'

'Good. Dress informal. Seven-thirty.'

I returned to the sitting-room.

Eyes closed, Frank was blissfully imagining the many opportunities he would have to bring up the subject of the account.

It was as well his eyes were closed so that he couldn't see Madge's expression: it was how Delilah must have looked when she picked up the razor.

'The arrogant old bitch,' she said.

Frank's eyes snapped open. 'What do you mean, honey?' he wailed.

'She thinks everybody will jump when she gives the word.'

When $20,000,000 gave the word.

'But, honey, you said you'd go.'

'I did not.'

'But you didn't say you wouldn't go.'

'You must go, Madge,' I said, sternly. 'I've accepted on your behalf.'

'Don't worry, Dad. I want to tell that fat old cow what I think of her.'

Frank was bewildered. What was the Lord up to? He had melted Madge's obduracy but seemed at the same time to have put some sinister intention in her mind.

I had the same fear. 'I'd rather you didn't go, Madge, if you intend to make a scene. Remember, Frank's career could be at stake.'

'So it could, honey,' said Frank.

Madge then looked shifty and, dear God, was more than ever like her mother, who had never looked shifty in her life.

'Is that what you both think of me?' she asked haughtily. 'I don't know how to behave myself as a guest in a house that cost three million?'

'It's worth more than that now,' said Frank wistfully.

9

Frank could not have been more excited if it had been the Governor of the Bank of Heaven that he was going to visit. What jacket, what bow tie, what pants, what shoes should he wear? Should he take with him his diplomas, certificates, and testimonials? At what point, with what approach, should he bring up the subject of the Account? Now and then amidst his babbling he would lapse into a dwam, with a dull sad look in his eyes, as if a sackful of dollars had fallen on him from a great height.

Was he in trouble at the bank? Had he committed some blunder by which a few million had been lost? Had his employers told him that he had reached the limits of his money-making capacity and could expect no further promotion? Unless, of course, he won the patronage of some rich stockholder such as Mrs Birkenberger.

Madge wore a black dress, bought, she reminded me, to mourn her mother. Her handbag was also black. In it, her smile hinted, could be a gun with which she intended to assassinate her hostess. That was an absurd fantasy on my part and yet, here in California, guns of all kinds could be bought in pawn-shops.

We set out shortly after seven, Frank driving the Oldsmobile. Madge sat beside him. I was in the back. It was a half-hour's journey: in California almost next door.

The evening was warm and pleasant. In Lunderston it would be three in the morning, and probably dull, cold, and wet. How were they all getting on in my absence? As well as they did when I was there. Already I would not be missed. People were too content with their own stay-at-home existences to envy any traveller. It would be the same when I was dead and gone for good.

I remembered Kate and sighed.

'What's the matter, Dad?' asked Madge. 'You're the guest of honour, remember. So no sulking, please.'

'When did I ever sulk?'

'Every time you didn't get your own way.'

I pretended she meant it as a joke, and let it pass.

'We know she's half Mexican,' said Madge, 'but what's the other half? No one knows.'

'That's no one's business but hers,' said Frank manfully.

'Isn't it awful how films and television have made people with tiny talents rich and famous? Don't you agree, Dad?'

I had to. She had heard me say it often.

'Of course her boobs were never tiny, or her ass.'

'If you're going to be vulgar, Madge,' I said, 'at least be honest about it. "Arse" is the word, not "ass".'

Madge laughed. '"Arse" sounds more like it. I wonder how many men she's had in her bed. Fifty? A hundred?'

'Please don't talk like that, honey,' said Frank.

'And what about the young studs they say she hires? It's bad enough a man paying for sex, it's a lot worse a woman doing it, especially if she's old and ought to be past it.'

All passion spent, as Milton had put it. But, if it applied to Linda, it must also apply to me.

'To tell you the truth,' said Madge, 'I'm more interested in her housekeeper, the murderess.'

'But, honey, haven't I heard you say she was right to shoot him? Didn't you say that, if anyone raped Midge, you'd shoot him?'

That silenced Madge for the rest of the journey.

The gates opened mysteriously as we approached. We drove through the grounds.

The house and garden, Frank reminded us, had been used many years ago in the film *Lost Souls*, in which Linda Blossom had starred. It had been shown on television recently. The scene in which she had walked among these statues and bushes with the dead baby in her arms was terrific.

'Isn't it odd,' said Madge, 'that in spite of all those marriages she's never had any children?'

'It never pleased the good Lord to make her fruitful,' said Frank.

'It pleased Him to make her very rich.'

'Isn't she to be pitied, having all that money and yet never knowing the joy of motherhood?'

'What joy? She's to be envied.'

'You don't mean that, honey.'

'It's disgraceful that a woman like her should own a place like this. No wonder there are Communists.'

Our hostess came down the terrace steps to greet us. She wore a white silk cheongsam, suitable for a shapely girl of 17, not a woman of 70 with bulges. It was so tight round her hips and bosom that she shuffled and gasped. A comb glittered in her hair. Were there diamonds? Her face was white with powder, her mouth as red as the dragon on her dress. She was grotesque and yet, it seemed to me, beautiful.

It would have been absurd for me, at my age and still grieving for Kate, to be falling in love. Yet I had a warm feeling for her, which could have been affection.

She smiled graciously at Frank's fawning, was amused by Madge's haughtiness, and, to my annoyance, addressed me as 'Mr Casaubon', the sexless clergyman in *Middlemarch*.

We sat on the terrace and the Chinese servant Chung took our orders for drinks. I wondered again, was he a eunuch? Once, in a film set in ancient Greece, Linda had been part princess and part goddess, with eunuchs to soap her in her bath. In the script, there had been lines satirical of their inability to give a woman another

109

kind of pleasure and she had delivered them with an earthy gusto unbefitting her divinity. As a consequence, the film had been an international box-office success. She had also, I recalled, starred in a film as an Eastern princess rescued from the clutches of a lecherous sheik by a band of intrepid catamites.

Madge wanted only mineral water to drink, Frank Coca-Cola. I asked for scotch and was given the finest I had ever tasted. In golf clubs all over Scotland, connoisseurs speak with reverence of whiskies so rare that only Texan oilmen and Arab princes could afford them. Here was such a one. Not even Linda's persistence in calling me Mr Casaubon could spoil its savour.

Madge and Frank must have thought she was drunkenly confusing me with one of her former lovers.

Even Madge was impressed by the display of opulence and good taste shown in the arrangements for the meal. The dishes were made in Sèvres. Vases of silver contained roses. The place mats had paintings by Velázquez. The table itself was of massive mahogany and the cloth covering it of finest damask. As for the food and drink, they were excellent. For all this, I was sure, the credit should go to Morland. Linda's own contribution was the background music, an excruciating mixture of banality and sentimentality, perpetrated by an aged bewigged crooner who had made millions out of it. Jerry was a personal friend, said Linda. She loved his singing.

Tactfully, I praised it.

'Don't be hypcritical, Dad,' said Madge. 'You hate pop music. When Jean and I were children, you wouldn't let us listen to it.'

I could have wrung her neck. She was making me out to be like Mr Casaubon, who also would have hated pop music.

'Well,' I said, feebly, 'I have to say, much of it does seem rather shallow and insincere, especially when the theme is love.'

Frank tried to help. 'Dad prefers the love songs of Robbie Burns. He's very good at singing them.'

'I didn't know you could sing, Mr Casaubon,' said Linda.

'In an amateurish kind of way,' I said.

'You'll have to sing for me.'

'He plays the piano too,' said Frank.

'Not to mention the bagpipes,' I said ironically.

'Don't boast, Dad,' said Madge. 'When you've had too much to drink, you always start boasting.'

Linda decided to defend me. Unfortunately, she chose to do it offensively. Perhaps she didn't think she was being offensive; she thought she was being honest.

'Well, what's wrong with that?' she demanded. 'I don't expect you've got anything to boast about, Mrs Sourpuss. Or this pious prick either.'

She meant Frank, but had she said 'prick'? Could it have been 'prig'? But Americans, like the Scots, rarely used that word. It was peculiar to the English, who had so many of them. To be fair, it was as good a description of Frank as any, and Mrs Sourpuss suited Madge.

'The world's full of jealous bastards,' said Linda. 'Look at all the garbage they've dug up about me, most of it lies. Why? Because I won the jackpot and they got peanuts.'

'Such people are not true Americans,' said Frank solemnly. 'Because of your talents your films were successful, so it was only right and proper that you should have been richly rewarded.'

Linda laughed. 'What talents, for Chrissake? A pair of big tits, a cute ass, and a laugh that made the guys want to screw me and the dames want to scratch my eyes out.'

After the meal, on our way out of the dining-room, Madge whispered to me, 'Look out, Dad. She's laughing at you all the time. She thinks you're an impostor.'

'An impostor? In what way an impostor?'

'Putting on airs as if you were as rich as her, when all you've got is a headmaster's pension.'

'Is money all that matters?'

'Don't be stupid, Dad. Of course it is. People like her have got lots of hangers-on.'

Yes, but I wasn't just any ordinary hanger-on. Was I not Mr Casaubon?

I went over to the piano and began to amuse myself by playing a medley of Burns's songs.

Linda was sitting beside Frank on a sofa. He was talking seriously. This, at last, was his opportunity. She seemed to be paying heed.

Madge, seated apart, smiled and scowled in turns. Such was her mood the scowls became her, the smiles didn't.

'Sing me a love-song by Robbie Burns, Mr Casaubon,' salled Linda.

'I doubt if Mr Casaubon ever heard of Robert Burns.'

'Sing one anyway.'

'Very well. "Ae Fond Kiss" it shall be.'

'For heaven's sake, Dad,' said Madge, 'remember where you are.'

She meant in plutocratic California, where the songs of an Ayrshire farmer who had made not a penny out of them were hardly likely to be appreciated.

'If I were among the Inuits of Canada or the Tamils of Southern India, this song would not be out of place. Its appeal is universal.'

I had drunk just the right amount to be able to sing with the right degree of pathos that most moving song of lost love.

As I sang, I recalled that the love affair that had inspired the song, that between Burns and his Clarinda, alias Mrs McIlhose, respectable Edinburgh housewife, had not lasted long and had elements of comedy in it.

My mood therefore was more ironic than mawkish. So I was astonished when suddenly I was overwhelmed by a great sadness. My fingers on the keys stopped, my voice faltered. I was in tears.

There was silence.

'I warned you, Dad,' said Madge. 'You've drunk too much.'

'He's thinking of your mother, you dumb bitch,' cried Linda.

So I was, and of my own mother, dead almost 50 years. The wrongs I had done them, never now to be remedied, would fester in my soul until I died. But these tears were not only of guilt, grief caused them too, and a sense of my own inadequacy.

Linda brought to me a glass of Drambuie. In her eyes I could see that she did indeed regard me as an impostor, but of a more interesting kind than she had supposed.

'Thank you, Linda,' I said. 'Sorry about that. Don't know what came over me.'

'I know. It happens to me often.'

'I'm afraid I don't feel like singing. Another time perhaps.'

'Sure, another time. What I heard was beautiful.' She bent and kissed me on the cheek.

We left about an hour later. Linda saw us off. She put her head into the car. 'Make sure you win the Cup tomorrow.'

'Knowing that you are to present it will make me try all the harder.'

She laughed, raucous as a peacock.

We heard her all the way to the gates.

'What a dreadful woman,' said Madge, but she wasn't so sure now.

'She listened to me,' said Frank, 'and asked some very pertinent questions.'

'She's senile,' said Madge. 'Look how she kept calling Dad Mr Casaubon.'

'I wonder who Mr Casaubon was. Sounds like a Frenchman. Do you know, Dad?'

It was Linda's secret and mine. 'I think it was just a little joke on her part.'

'A silly little joke,' said Madge.

So silly that once or twice I had been on the point of

retaliating by calling her Dorothea, for I was no more like Casaubon than she was like Dorothea.

It happens to me often, she had said. What had she meant? Did she too have terrifying moments of guilt, grief, and inadequacy?

Perhaps, if our friendship ripened, we could help each other to face the truth and be happy in spite of it, in our final days.

10

Only 15 took part in the over-70s competition for the Birkenberger Cup. There had been 18 names on the sheet but two had to withdraw because their legs, literally, had let them down, and the third had expired in the interim, while practising putting on the carpet at home. Jests were made on the subject of old Silas's last putt, but there was a minute's silence on the first tee in his honour, during which the remaining contestants, including myself, wondered when the Great Starter in the sky would call out their names.

It was a stroke competition. Every player who managed to complete the round would deduct his handicap from his score and the result would be what counted. Mine was the lowest handicap at eight. The highest was 30. That meant I had to give starts, as it were, of up to 22 strokes. Usually this would have been almost impossible, but here those with the highest handicaps were so frail that their electric carts were really ambulances. Small wonder, therefore, that the event was a source of wisecracks. It would have been scrapped from the calendar years ago but for fear of offending the patroness who happened also to be the landlady.

The custom was to have players with the lowest handicaps playing together. My partner, therefore, was Vic, aged 76, an ex-actor, who wore red-and-white bloomers. His handicap of 12 was, I suspected, false: it should have been nearer 20. As they grow older and stiffer, golfers hate their handicaps to rise, for it amounts to an admission to the whole world that their prowess, not only as a golfer, has declined and will go on declining. Consequently, they do everything they can, short of downright cheating, to avoid having their handicaps raised. This, of course, lessens their chances of winning, but assuages their pride. Vic was an example. Thus, my likeliest rival had eliminated himself from the outset.

The course was easy for me, in that it had hardly any rough, only grass a little longer than that on the fairway, whereas at Lunderston I was used to heather, blaeberry, bracken, ferns, wild flowers, and whins. Also, for this competition the course had been shortened. Above all I had the incentive that Linda was to present the Cup to the winner.

There are few satisfactions in life sweeter than that of a golfer who has just hit a good shot. He feels, as the ball soars high and far in the right direction or stops on the green a frog's leap from the hole, that living is worth-while, people are decent, the poor and the sick will win through, and Armageddon will be a long time coming. If his playing partner should shout, 'Great shot!', or some chance spectator sees and applauds, it adds a little to his joy but it is not necessary. It is essentially a private experience, like communion with God.

During that round, I felt that mystical joy many times. I would have hesitated to say that those four hours were the happiest of my life, for there had been my wooing of Kate, my service in the war, the births of my children, my year as captain of Lunderston Golf Club, when a prince had been entertained, and the five occasions when I had won the club championship; but all those previous triumphs had had in them some small element of detraction, whereas that round of golf, that sunny Sunday morning, was pure bliss.

My score was 71. With my handicap deducted, I had a net return of 63. Since the next net score was 76, I had won by 13 strokes. It was unprecedented.

Nevertheless, the chief subject of conversation in the clubhouse that afternoon was not my outstanding victory but Linda's appearance. When word had spread that she was going to present the prizes this year, there had been grumbles and misgivings. It was a ceremony for a lady. The dignity of the Club would suffer. But from the minute she stepped out of the Cadillac, she comported herself so well that even those who resented her most were at a loss to find fault. They were reduced to jeering that it wasn't natural, it was all put on: an absurd objection, for civilised behaviour on anyone's part demands conscious effort.

She was dressed appropriately for the occasion. Instead of her usual gaudy dress or blouse low at the neck and high at the thigh, she wore a white linen suit of chaste length, pink blouse, pink shoes with heels of reasonable height, pink stockings, and earrings that, though consisting of rubies, were not too ostentatious. Her hair, black as ever, was arranged in a style suited to her mature age. Her perfume was delicious and discreet.

Evidently, she had been advised by Morland.

So far so good, they thought; but just wait till she opens her mouth. To the amazement and incredulity of those doubters and ill-wishers, when she spoke, it was quietly and articulately, in imitation, some thought, of the 'Queen of England', but really as I alone knew, of Dorothea Brooke, heroine of *Middlemarch*. No one but me noticed her swift wink as she handed me the Cup. 'I take great pleasure, Mr Casaubon' – here the Club captain had to correct her – 'Oh, I'm so sorry. I take great pleasure, Mr McLeod, in presenting you with this trophy, which everybody tells me is very well deserved, for you played brilliantly.' She bent forward to let me kiss her cheek. 'See you tonight, champion,' she whispered, as they all clapped. There was to be champagne for everybody, at her expense.

When she was gone, for, wisely, she did not linger, the talk was all about her transformation. My victory was forgotten. Had she decided after all to marry the English lord with whose name hers had been linked for some time, and had this afternoon's performance been a kind of rehearsal? Was she hoping to be presented to the 'Queen of England' when the latter visited California next spring? Was it some kind of religious conversion? If it was true that she had been born a Catholic, she must believe in hell whether she wanted to or not and, at her age, she hadn't much time to mend her ways to prevent her going there.

My own explanation would have been very different. It would never have been believed, so I kept it to myself. Linda had behaved like a lady in my honour. Her calling me Casaubon had been no slip. It had been a signal that only I could decode. She had been reminding me that she and I shared a secret. We might well share others. What had I to look forward to that night?

11

Frank clasped the Cup in his arms as if it was the Holy Grail. The smell of champagne off it did not repel him. Such a solid mass of silver must be worth thousands of dollars.

'I don't get it to keep, Frank,' I said. 'Just for a month. Then it goes back into the showcase, with my name inscribed on it.'

'Aren't you proud of your Dad, honey?'

'Did she really present it herself?' asked Madge.

'She did, with great charm.'

'We ought to have been there,' said Frank.

' "With great charm"?' said Madge. 'Do you expect us to believe that?'

'Yes, because it's the truth. Ask anyone who was there. By the way, I'm invited to dinner tonight.'

'By yourself?'

'Yes. A prerogative of the winner.'

Frank did not mean to titter. Nervousness caused it. Although no one at the Club told him scurrilous stories, for he was known not to be that kind of man, he must have overheard some, for he was also that kind of man and, therefore, he knew what was said about Linda and the winner of the Cup.

'Well, you can't go,' said Madge.

'Why can't I?'

'Because you promised to come to church with us. We've told Pastor Snodgrass you were coming.'

Perhaps I had given such a promise when feeling sorry for them, but it would have to be some other Sunday.

119

'Didn't he promise, Frank?' cried Madge.

In church I could do nothing about the account except pray, which Frank himself could do much better. In Linda's bed, I might do much. Thus Frank cogitated.

'To be fair, honey, I don't think Dad meant any particular Sunday.'

'Yes, he did. He meant tonight. He puts that outrageous woman before us.'

'Don't look at it like that, honey.'

'I know why you're taking his part, Frank. You're obsessed by money.'

'Not obsessed, honey. I just have a proper respect for it. Remember what Pastor Snodgrass said? Money well spent is faith in action. It builds churches. It feeds the poor. It brings sinners to Christ.'

'One of these days, Frank, do you know what I'm going to do? I'm going to tell Pastor Snodgrass to kiss my arse.'

With that, she ran out of the room.

Like a bad actress in a bad play, I thought.

'She doesn't mean it, Dad,' said Frank.

'I hope not, Frank. Literally, anyway.'

I didn't approve of my daughter using such a vulgar expression but, on the other hand, I felt rather pleased that she was showing signs of the free-thinking independence that I had tried to instil into her and her sister when they were young. Also she had used the stalwart honest word 'arse' and not the feeble substitute 'ass'.

An hour or so later Frank came to say that they were leaving for church. As elders, they had to be there early.

'Madge wants to know if you're coming.'

'Sorry, not this time.'

'Please give Mrs B. our regards.'

'I'll do that, Frank.'

'If you judge her to be in a sympathetic mood—'

'When the time's ripe, I'll mention it.'

'Thank you, Dad, and good luck.'

But what would constitute good luck in my dealings with Linda that night? Going to bed with her? Yes, but suppose I failed to perform to her satisfaction, suppose, in golfing terms, I duffed my drives and missed my putts? Linda would take no limp excuses or give second chances.

12

I got out of the car and went up the terrace steps nimbly, pretending that my legs weren't weary and aching from the golf that morning. Unfortunately, Linda wasn't there to see and be impressed. Ms Morland was there in her place, but she looked concerned, as if she saw me as a decrepit old man, ready to collapse. Yet I was smartly dressed, in the Lunderston Golf Club blazer, red cravat, tan slacks, and Italian shoes.

It was really the first time I had seen her as a person in her own right, and not as Linda's housekeeper. I had never given a thought, either, to what her opinion of me might be.

She came up to me. 'May I speak to you for a moment, Mr McLeod?' she asked.

I hadn't realised how tall she was, and how handsome. There, among the flowers on the lamplit terrace, she looked strange and beautiful.

'Of course,' I said.

'Do you intend to spend Christmas in San Diego?'

I was taken aback. Was she carrying out some order of Linda's? Had she been given the job of dismissing me?

'Yes, that's my intention,' I said. 'I hope to spend Christmas with my daughter and her family.'

'In San Diego? Many people go away for Christmas.'

'I think they'll be spending it at home, in San Diego. Ms Morland, is there any special purpose in these questions? Are you asking them on behalf of Mrs Birkenberger?'

'No. She doesn't know. I would be grateful if you did not tell her.'

'Are you trying to give me some kind of warning?' I asked, but not angrily. Whatever she was, she was no jealous mischief-maker.

'Yes, Mr McLeod, I am.'

I felt a shudder of apprehension. She must have seen what had happened to other elderly wooers or fortune-hunters. In what category did she put me?

I saw myself as Ulysses on his travels, being warned by this part woman, part goddess, about the ogress into whose clutches he was about to fall. But had he not been wily as well as daring?

'Thank you, Ms Morland,' I said, 'but I think I can look after myself.'

Suddenly she changed her smile and tone of voice. From looking and sounding anxious, she looked and sounded amused.

'Mrs Birkenberger has arranged an entertainment for you, Mr McLeod. She hopes you will agree to take part.'

'What kind of entertainment? Will it be safe for me to take part?'

'Yes, of course. It has to do with the novel *Middlemarch*. Please come with me.'

She led me to a bedroom. On the bed, clothes were spread out. Looking closer, I saw that it was male evening dress of a past era, striped black trousers, black jacket, red silk waistcoat, and stiff white shirt with stiff collar.

'Have I to wear these?' I asked, not really objecting. I thought I would look well in them, even if they gave off a strong smell of mothballs.

'Is it some kind of play?' I asked.

She handed me a sheet of paper. On it was handwritten:

Scene 1. Dining-room of Lady Madeleine, widowed society lady and great-aunt of Miss Dorothea Brooke. Lady Madeleine is entertaining Sir Jasper, a nobleman. They have met to discuss the forthcoming marriage of Miss Brooke to the Rev. Edward Casaubon.

Scene 2. The wedding-night of Miss Brooke and Mr Casaubon.

Good for Linda, I thought. What an original and enterprising approach to literary criticism.

'Is this Mrs Birkenberger's own idea?' I asked.

'Yes. If you need help with the clothes, please ring for Chung.'

'Thank you. I think I can manage.'

'When you are dressed, please go to the dining-room. Mrs Birkenberger will join you there.'

I felt peckish. 'Will we eat there?'

'Yes. Good luck.'

She smiled and then left.

As I put on the clothes, a strange thing happened. The more I looked like Sir Jasper, the more I felt like him. It was a haughty 19th-century aristocrat who gazed back at me in the mirror.

On my way to the dining-room, I took a carnation from a vase and put it in my buttonhole.

As I made my entrance, I imagined that there was an audience watching, so I advanced with histrionic elegance. Nonchalantly, I went to the sideboard and poured myself a dram. Glass in hand, I strolled around, looking at the paintings on the walls, by Matisse and Monet and others, anachronisms, of course, for they hadn't been painted at the time of the events related in *Middlemarch*.

The door opened and in came not Mrs Birkenberger, but Lady Madeleine. She moved with grace, though her red velvet dress trailed on the carpet. Much of her bosom was exposed, but fashion, not sexual flaunting, was the cause. To achieve the small waist of the period, a strong corset was evidently in use. She glittered with jewellery.

How would she choose to speak?

'My apologies, Sir Jasper, for keeping you waiting.'

Her imitation of an upper-class English accent was very good. It wouldn't be me who would win the Oscar.

'May I offer you a preprandial refreshment, my dear?' I asked.

'How very kind of you, Sir Jasper.'

Linda would have wanted a large scotch. Madeleine got a small sherry.

'You received my message, Jasper?'

'Yes, indeed. So your nice Dorothea Brooke is to marry Casaubon?'

'I am quite disappointed. In my opinion, he is not suitable.'

'In what respect? I understand he has a handsome fortune.'

'She is only nineteen. He is fifty, at least. Besides, he is a clergyman.'

'Do not clergymen make respectable if dull husbands? Dorothea herself, I believe, is inclined to gravity.'

'He does not enjoy good health. He is engaged upon a work of useless and tedious scholarship. Dorothea is too dutiful. She wishes to sacrifice her life to nursing him and assisting him in his dreary labours.'

'But is she not fond of him?'

'Who could be fond of such a desiccated creature?'

'What, then, is her purpose in marrying him?'

'No one knows. It is a mystery. All her friends are appalled, particularly Sir James Chettam, to whom her sister Celia is married.'

'To my knowledge, Sir James is a gentleman of good sense and judgment. If he does not approve, then the situation is in truth alarming.'

'He certainly does not approve.'

'If your niece had been an empty-headed impulsive girl, I might have understood, but I have always heard her spoken of as deliberate and clever.'

126

Sir Jasper then took Lady Madeleine's hand and whispered into her sparkling ear, 'Can it be that she has some hidden motive for consenting to this marriage? Can it be that she is hopeful that the stresses of married life will hasten his departure to partake of the rewards promised the godly? And, alas, leave her here on earth to enjoy his fortune?'

While Linda, or Lady Madeleine, was looking astonished at that imputation, which wasn't as it were, in the script, the door opened and in came servants carrying dishes. They were careful not to giggle. They must have been warned that they mustn't.

Lady Madeleine and Sir Jasper took their places at the table. He was pleased to see that the wine was good and plentiful, as also was the food.

'You have disturbed me, Sir Jasper. Dorothea is a girl of honour. She would not sell herself for money.'

'Let us be honest, Madeleine. Do not all girls of our class sell themselves for money? Mama makes it clear that the comforts and privileges they enjoy as ladies must be paid for. Papa can no longer afford to, so husband must. Dorothea has neither Mama to advise her nor Papa to support her, so, like the astute resolute girl she is, she has decided on Casaubon; and there is something else which she has taken into consideration.'

'And what is that, pray?'

'From what I have heard of your niece, she is more cerebral than romantic by nature. She has perceived that, as a husband, Casaubon will make few demands upon her. I refer to the physical obligations of marriage. Probably he will make none at all. Robuster girls might pine, but Dorothea will, no doubt, rejoice.'

Lady Madeleine's face had been getting redder by the minute and she'd begun to gasp.

'The marriage-bed should be a place of joy and discovery,' said Sir Jasper. 'Theirs, I fear, will be bleak and barren.'

'For God's sake, cut,' yelled Linda, very much in her own

voice. 'I'll have to get out of this fucking straitjacket before I faint.'

She rushed, panting, out of the room.

I helped myself to more wine. I felt confident. The Oscar, after all, was mine.

When she returned, she was noticeably fatter. 'Thank God for that,' she cried. 'Now I can enjoy my dinner. God knows how those dames put up with it.'

'For the sake of appearance, Linda, women throughout the ages have been prepared to suffer a great deal of discomfort.'

'The game's over, Professor, for now. You were good. You'd have done well in movies. That's not all compliment. You've to have a lot of the phony in you to do well in movies.'

Again, that insinuation of falseness. I let it pass.

'You were very good yourself, Linda.'

'I was an actress, remember, and I did some rehearsing. Sarah supplied me with some lines. Tell me, were you serious about Dorothea having married Casaubon for his money? I don't remember that being mentioned in the book.'

'But, Linda, the book's permeated by money. All those substantial fortunes. All those delightful estates. Sustained, of course, by servants little better than serfs.'

'I guess so. The way they visited the poor, thinking themselves so superior, it'd make you puke. Yeah, I guess you're right, Professor, Dorothea had her eye on Casaubon's money without knowing it.'

'Oh, I think she knew it all right.'

'All those fine ladies and gentlemen, they were nothing but fucking parasites.'

I was surprised by her vehemence.

'Something else you said, Professor. About the marriage-bed being a place of joy and discovery. I don't know about the joy but it sure can be a place of discovery.'

I poured myself more wine.

'Don't drink too much, Professor. Scene two's coming up.'

'Set in the marriage-bed?'

'That's right.'

'Your bed, Linda?'

'Dorothea's bed. It might have to be X-rated.' She laughed. 'Sarah's looked out a nightshirt and a nightcap for you. I'll be wearing drawers. Did you know that well-brought-up ladies went to bed wearing drawers?'

13

Wearing a nightshirt down to my ankles and a nightcap with a tassel, I waited for my cue. In the mirror there was Casaubon, looking very uneasy. Under the nightshirt was Casaubon too, ominously inert.

The telephone rang. 'You may come now, Mr Casaubon.'

It was the voice of a young girl, prim but resolute.

The room was lit by a single candle. There were shadows and dark places. Linda was in bed, wearing a white bonnet and a nightgown buttoned up to the chin. I couldn't, of course, tell if she was wearing drawers.

I was so conscious of poor Casaubon's predicament that it was my predicament too. Whose now was the inertness?

As I felt my way towards the bed, I stubbed my toes against the leg of a chair. I had to suffer in silence, though the pain was considerable.

What put it into my head to say as I approached the bed, 'We must pray, my dear'? Was it to mock Casaubon or to be true to him? He would have said it out of piety but also to put off for a little longer the ordeal before him.

Dorothea would not have objected but Linda did. 'Is it necessary?'

'Yes, my dear, we must ask the Lord's blessing.'

'Must I get out of bed?'

'To be efficacious, prayer must not be done lying in comfort. It must be done on one's knees, as a token of humility.'

With a Linda-ish grunt, Dorothea got out of bed and knelt

131

beside it. On the other side, I knelt too. We clasped our hands.

'What do we pray for, Mr Casaubon?' she muttered.

What indeed? Casaubon would hardly have thanked the Lord for what he dreaded to take, nor would he have pleaded for the Lord's help, not wishing to involve that chastest of celibates. Other men might have asked to be blessed with children, but not Casaubon. I couldn't see him as a father. To be fair, I couldn't see Dorothea as a mother.

As for Dorothea's thoughts, they were Linda's business.

To be on the safe side, I made it silent prayer. I made it last five minutes. After all, Casaubon would have made it last twenty.

We both rose stiffly, she with murmurs of resentment: poor acting, I thought. Dorothea would never have uttered them.

When she was back in bed, I was about to follow her when she said, 'Remember your medicine, Mr Casaubon. It is on the table beside the candle.'

It looked and, as I soon found out, smelled, as if it would have a horrible taste. Was this Linda's idea of a joke or Dorothea's wifely solicitude? In the book, Casaubon's medicine was mentioned.

I took a sip, for art's sake. It was nauseating.

'You must take it all, Mr Casaubon. That's what the doctor said.'

'Yes, my dear.' I was speaking with Casaubon's voice, a self-pitying feeble whine. I drank it all. I felt like vomiting. My toes ached.

'You may come to bed now, Mr Casaubon.'

My bones, acting their part well, creaked as I climbed into the bed. I lay well apart from her. Casaubon, poor bugger, would have bartered his soul to be allowed to go chastely to sleep.

'You have forgotten to extinguish the candle, Mr Casaubon.'

Casaubon would have wanted to keep it lit. Seen, this woman now his wife, would be terrifying; unseen, even worse. Obediently I leant out and blew out the candle. It took me, as Casaubon, five asthmatic puffs.

We lay in silence. There was a noise. It was Linda's stomach rumbling. Gregor McLeod grinned at that, but Casaubon wouldn't have. But then Dorothea's stomach wouldn't have rumbled.

'Mr Casaubon?' It was Dorothea speaking.

'Yes, my dear?'

'Is there not something we should do?'

'What do you mean?'

'To establish our union in the eyes of God, ought we not to be made one flesh? Is not that the purpose of marriage?'

This was Linda the actress at her best.

I did not let her down. 'I believe so, my dear.'

'It is not enough to hold hands?'

'No, that is not enough.'

'What then, Mr Casaubon?'

'Could it not be deferred, my dear? We are both worn out with the day's events.'

'It cannot be deferred. This is our wedding-night. The sacrament must be completed now. I think that is the custom.'

'Yes, my dear, that is the custom.'

'What is it that has to be done?'

'Has not your sister Celia, who is married, or Mrs Cadwallader, the rector's wife, advised you, my dear?'

'Ladies do not discuss such matters, Mr Casaubon.'

'If your dear mother had not passed away—'

'My mother was a lady, Mr Casaubon. She would not have discussed it either.'

Casaubon would not have discussed it with God.

'As a clergyman, Mr Casaubon, to whom people come for counsel, were you not, at College, equipped with such knowledge?'

Casaubon was not so equipped and no one had ever had the temerity to consult him on such a subject.

'But, Mr Casaubon, we are country people. We see the cock among his hens, the bull among his cows.'

Linda, I thought, you're stretching it.

'So we have an idea of what is to be done?'

'Yes, my dear.'

'Then let us proceed. It will be necessary for me to remove my drawers.'

'I fear so, my dear.'

Quickly they were removed and thrown out of the bed.

Whether as Casaubon or Gregor McLeod, I was in need of stimulation. Casaubon would never have sought it from Dorothea and Gregor could not expect it from Linda.

Whose hand then, Linda's or Dorothea's, that pulled up the nightshirt – whose nightshirt? – and took hold of – Casaubon was it? Or Gregor?

Would virginal Dorothea have done this? Yes, if she thought it was customary.

But would Casaubon have placed his hand, sanctioned by God, on the corresponding part of Dorothea?

I expected her to shout, 'Cut!' and push me out of the bed. But no, she pulled me up on top of her and made what followed easy for me; well, not easy, but not impossibly difficult.

I gave myself four out of ten for performance, nine out of ten for effort.

She said nothing till it was over.

'You have over-exerted yourself, Mr Casaubon. From now on, we must be abstinent.'

'Dear Dorothea,' I gasped, 'does not improvement come with practice?'

Her laughter then could never have been mistaken for Dorothea's.

14

I stayed the night, but not in Linda's bed. She preferred to sleep alone. I wasn't to feel offended. She had never let any of her husbands spend a whole night in bed with her. She liked to be able to toss and turn and have nightmares, but she hinted that there was another reason which she had told no one and wasn't going to tell me either.

For a while I lay awake smoking a cigar and assessing my progress. On the whole, it was satisfactory. I had done as well as Casaubon. Linda had praised my performance. I had made love to her. True, it was supposed to have been Casaubon making love to Dorothea, but the bodies had been mine and Linda's. I hadn't done all that well, managing a mere pass, but I had genuine excuses, that horrible medicine (the taste still lingered), my skinned toes (now covered with sticking plaster), and my having to be fair to Casaubon. The next time – surely that bawdy laughter had promised me a second attempt – I ought to do better. Perhaps there would be fondness between us then.

I had qualms. She had not got her reputation for fierceness for nothing. I had already suffered a few mental lacerations. Her wealth gave her power and, of course, power corrupted. One word to the president of the bank and Frank was out of a job.

Breakfast was served beside the pool. I had been there, alone, except for some butterflies, for nearly half an hour before my hostess appeared, wearing loose yellow slacks and a pink blouse. She had not yet applied make-up, as if she did not mind my seeing her wrinkles and blotches. We were, in that respect, like a married couple; and like a married couple too in another respect. Until I had gauged her mood, I had to be careful not to provoke her.

'Good morning, Professor,' she said, as she sat down.

At least I was no longer Mr Casaubon.

She poured herself coffee. She drank it black. She didn't seem to want anything to eat.

In a bush nearby a hummingbird was sucking nectar out of flowers. Its place in the universe was secure. If there was a God, He loved it.

Linda was looking at me as I had been looking at the bird. Was she questioning my place, not in the universe, but in her life.

'Tell me, Professor' she said, 'if you wrote your life story, would you tell the whole truth?'

I was taken aback. Was she going to pry into my secrets?

'No one would give tuppence for my life story,' I said.

'I've been offered half a million dollars for mine.'

Some professional hack would do it for her. It would be trivial and dull, but it would make more money than a dozen works of literature.

'Well, Professor, would you?'

'Isn't it well-nigh impossible to tell the whole truth about oneself?'

'Why is it impossible? You know what happened. So you tell it as it happened.'

'I don't think it's as simple as that.'

'Not if you keep trying to hide things, or make them better than they were.'

'Haven't we all a right to keep our secrets?'

With her elbow on the table, she rested her chin on her hand and stared at me. 'You interest me, Professor,' she said.

I smiled. 'Well, that's flattering.'

'Maybe not so flattering. Some weeks ago, I nearly got myself married to an English lord: Lord Buckford. He's really an old bum who's been hanging about Beverly Hills for years, sponging on everybody, but he's a genuine lord, though his estates were sold long ago. No chin but loads of class. No brains either, but you just had to see him drinking someone else's brandy to know that his class was the real McCoy. Now yours, Professor, is imitation; very good imitation, in some ways better than the real thing.'

I laughed. 'I don't know what you're talking about, Linda.'

'I'm an expert on phonies, Professor. All my life I've been surrounded by them. A long time ago, when it was reported in a magazine that my father had taken a powder the day I was born and had never showed up since, do you know how many crawled out of the woodwork claiming to be him? Twenty-four.'

'Perhaps one of them was genuine, Linda.'

'Not a chance. The story wasn't true anyway. My father ran off months before I was born. So I never knew him. Don't feel hurt, Professor, if I place you among the phonies. You're a sort I've never met before. The worst phony I've ever known was me. I had to be at the beginning and it became a habit. I used to think that, when I had enough money, I wouldn't give a damn what anyone thought of me but, the more money I had, the phonier I became. I'd like to say this, though, that I've known when I was being a phony, not to mention a bitch and a shit; not all of me, but too much of me. I've tried to put it down on paper. I'd like you to look at it, Professor, and say what you think.'

I could see dangers in such an undertaking, but opportunities too.

'Aren't there professional writers who specialise in such work?' I said.

'They turn out crap. I want my story to be like *Middlemarch*, serious and truthful.'

I blinked at that comparison. Yet Linda had more character than any of the ladies in that masterpiece, and her life had been a great deal more varied.

'I thought of asking Josh Bolton but he would have made it into his book and I want it to be mine. I think you and me understand each other, Professor.'

'I'll be delighted to help, Linda.'

'You'll not be doing it for nothing. Your fee would be ten thousand dollars now and ten thousand more when the book's published. If it's never published, for whatever reason, you'll still get the second ten thousand, provided it's me that gives up. You'll stay here, so that we can work on it whenever I feel like it. What do you say? Do you want time to think about it?'

'No need, Linda. I accept with pleasure.'

I was about to say that I didn't want any fee, the pleasure of her company would be payment enough, but I stopped myself in time. Anyone who didn't want money was automatically a phony.

'Good. I'll let you know when we start. Sarah will make the arrangements for your stay here. Consider yourself a guest, with free run of the place.'

'Thank you, Linda.'

She got up then and left.

I telephoned Madge.

'You didn't come home last night, Dad. I waited up for you. I was afraid you might have been in an accident.'

'I'm sorry, Madge.'

'Did you stay with her?'

'Well, in her house anyway. Don't be offended, Madge, but I'm going to be here for a few days.'

'With Mrs Birkenberger?'

'Yes. She's given me a job.'

'What kind of job?'

'She's written her memoirs and wants me to edit them.'

'Well, Dad, you've had plenty of experience correcting the work of dunces.'

I let that pass. 'I'll be along this afternoon to pick up my things.'

'Did you sleep with her, Dad?'

'Isn't that an improper question for a daughter to ask?'

'It's not me that wants to know. It's Frank. He's got it into his head that, if you were to ask about her account in bed, she'd be sure to let him have it. Very naive of him, wouldn't you say? Aren't people in bed at their most dishonest with each other? By the way, three letters have come for you. All from women. One's from Jean, so we won't count that. One's from Mrs Cramond, she's the widow you're supposed to be going on a world cruise with. The third one's from someone called Helen Sneddon. Who's she?'

'You met her at your mother's funeral. She's over 80 and married to Henry, who's also over 80.'

'Oh. Well, I'm working this afternoon, Dad. But you've got your own key. Keep in touch, will you?'

'Of course.'

'You'll find the letters on the dressing-table in your room.'

As I put the telephone down, I felt an access of paternal sympathy. Poor Madge had a lot to put up with: a pot-smoking son who failed his examinations, a daughter who slept around, a husband who mixed up Mammon and Christ, and a 72-year-old father on the make.

15

On the dressing-table were not only the three airmail letters, there was also a small unframed colour photograph which probably had been taken out of an album. It was some kind of appeal, but what was being asked of me?

It was of the two girls when children, and Kate when she was about 35. As always, she looked beautiful and eager. In the background was a Highland loch: Loch Broom, in Wester Ross. I remembered that cottage where we had spent a holiday. The wild roses had smelled fragrant because of the honeysuckle growing amongst them, and dolphins had leapt out of the water and fallen back again with loud slapping sounds heard half a mile away. A neighbour's son had sold us illicit salmon. There had been an apple tree in the stony garden. It had been a dry lavatory and I had had difficulty in burying the contents of the Elsanol can because it had been a rainless summer and the ground was hard as bone. The girls had covered their eyes as I had gone about with my spade looking for a soft spot. We had used bunches of meadowsweet as a deodorant.

The three of them were smiling at the man with the camera, myself, as I remembered, in khaki shorts.

I had been a good enough father, in that I had provided my family with a comfortable home and seen to it that they were fed and clothed as well as their neighbours. I had never been effusive in my display of fatherly affection, but then, what Scottish father ever was? And what Scottish daughters liked to be slobbered over?

All the same I had let pass many opportunities to show my love. That everybody did in no way lessened the regret. I could still make it up to my daughters, but not to Kate.

If challenged, I would have maintained, to Madge and Jean, and to their mother's ghost, that part of my reason for wanting to continue and perhaps deepen my friendship with Linda was that it would help me not to forget Kate, for I could never do that, but to save me from remembering her too often and therefore missing her too much. That way lay despair. Kate would have understood.

About halfway to Linda's I stopped at a wayside bar, where two white horses galloped about in a paddock. Under palm trees I would drink a cold beer and read my letters.

Jean's first. 'Madge tells us you're already well in with Mrs Birkenberger, who used to be the film star Linda Blossom. We saw one of her films on TV the other night. She was much younger then, of course, but there was a picture of her as she now is in the *Radio Times* and, to be fair, she's still a beautiful woman, though, of course, in the picture you couldn't see her wrinkles.

'What exactly *is* your connection with her, Dad? Robert and I think Madge has no right to try to live your life for you. You've always known what you were doing, haven't you? Robert and I have often commented on it. You've called yourself a socialist but you've never associated with that kind of riff-raff, it's always been with the people who matter. Just the same, Dad, take care that your acquaintance with Mrs Birkenberger doesn't interfere with your friendship with Mrs Cramond. Robert's done a wee bit of speiring, and Mrs Cramond is really well-off. Of course she's not nearly as rich as Mrs Birkenberger, but isn't hers fool's gold?

'Ian and Robin are doing well at school and send their love. We got the impression from Madge that her two aren't doing as well as she would like but you know Madge, hers have got to be

142

better than everybody else's. She was always a bit like that, but she's got worse from living in California.

'Take care of yourself, Dad. We all send our love. Write soon.'

The horses in the paddock were rubbing their heads together fondly.

Who, Jean, I asked aloud, are the people who matter?

I pictured her face if one day I turned up on the doorstep of her semi-detached villa in Morningside with Linda by my side and our Rolls at the gate.

I read Susan's next. Her handwriting was as firm as her voice. 'I have a feeling that, in spite of your promise, you'll not write to me, so here I am writing to you. I want to say that what happened between us after the party at my house committed you to nothing, though the offer still stands. I was in earnest but I felt you weren't. In any case, whatever happens, I want to tell you that the sight of you striding down Goatfell Avenue in rain or sunshine with your head in the air, swishing your stick and not giving a bugger for anyone, has often lifted my heart. Not only mine. I expect you knew you had all us widows at our windows when you came in sight. Dear Kate. I'm sure she knew she was sharing you with half a dozen of us at least but she was too generous to mind. God forgive me, I keep forgetting you lost her so recently. You must be missing her unbearably at times.

'As you know, I've got little small talk. I'll leave that to Helen. She'll give you all the gossip. She's the salt of the earth, I know, but I can't stand her. By the way, Henry was found dead the other day, where else but in the lavatory? Look after yourself.'

I noticed she had said nothing about Millie Tulloch. Was poor Millie's fate, whatever it was, to be included among the gossip?

I wasn't deceived by the apparently callous 'by the way' when she had mentioned Henry's death. It hadn't been Henry she was trying to dismiss as incidental, it was death itself. I remembered her terror – not too strong a word – at Kate's grave. But, Susan, there's nothing to be terrified about. For that's just what it is,

143

nothing. You go to sleep and never waken. What's so terrifying about that?

If that cruise ever takes place, we'll have a good time, you and I and Kate, for she'll be with us in our minds.

I was aware I had left someone out: Albert Cramond, Susan's husband, who had left her the money and the mansion. But she never spoke about him. He was, therefore, truly and conclusively dead.

Helen's letter was much the longest.

'To begin with, the weather's been vile – rain, sleet, and snow blowing in sheets off the Firth. We haven't seen the Arran hills for days. Everybody, including the dogs and cats, is full of aches and pains. Lucky you, basking in the warm sunshine.

'Sad news, Gregor. Henry's gone, dead and buried. Suddenly, though I'd been expecting it for years. He wanted a piper to play at his funeral. I asked Mr McFadyen of the Lunderston Pipe Band and he said he'd be pleased to play. So he did, in spite of the rain. It was very moving. There was quite a crowd in the kirkyard and outside it too. He also wanted his coffin to be wrapped in a Union Jack. Mr Gibb, the undertaker, wasn't very pleased. He seemed to think it was illegal. My consolation is that I won't be long after him.

'I noticed that Kate's headstone is at last in place. David Robertson took his time about it. But, to be fair, he's made a good job of it. There's room for your name, Gregor, though you've always said you'd be cremated. Where was it you told me you wanted your ashes to be scattered? On the thirteenth green, where you had a hole in one. But you were joking, weren't you?

'You'll want to know about Millie. Well, she's still in Laudermuir. I was going to visit her but, when I telephoned, they advised against it. She still refuses to speak to anyone. Would you believe it, Mrs Cardross is back in Colquhoun's, quite unashamed. Tulloch himself is back in his house, as if nothing had happened. What a mess folk make of their lives.

'More sad news, Gregor. I had a phone call from a friend who lives in Gantock, not far from your brother-in-law Mr Liddell. I'm sorry to have to tell you he's dead. The police had to break the door down to get in. He was found dead among his cats. I didn't really know him but I thought at Kate's funeral that I had never seen a more woebegone man. We all know that the human race will blow itself up one day but none of us thinks it will be our fault, so we don't worry about it. He worried too much.

'Mrs Borthwick, the big red-cheeked woman who worked in Murchison's, has got married, to someone called McCann. She helped at Susan's party, if you remember.

'I met Susan in the main street the other day. It was pouring, so we went into the Caledonian for a coffee. She looked quite unhappy. I really believe, Gregor, that she's missing you though, when I mentioned you, she changed the subject.

'No more news in the meantime.

'Take my advice, Gregor, and stay in the warmth as long as you can. But, when you come back, we'll all be glad to see you, those of us who are left. Maybe you weren't as fair to Kate as you might have been, and you've always been a wee bit of a show-off but, speaking for myself, I've always been fond of you and, when I remember you singing "Maiden of Morven", I'm afraid of nothing. So there's a confession from a daft old woman.

'Take care, as the Americans say. Tak tent, as the Scots used to say.'

As Helen's voice died away in my mind, I watched, through tears, the horses nuzzle each other. So Hector was dead. His body had not been dragged round the walls of grieving Troy by exultant Achilles but had been discreetly driven through the indifferent streets of his native town to the cemetery, among the trees, with no mourners, except perhaps for Chrissie Carruthers: an appropriate end for a man who did not want to be beholden.

Poor Millie. Silence could be noble and fruitful. Had I not

145

hankered after an ashram, where no one need speak? But not Millie's kind of silence. That did not come from an enriched soul but from one stunned by despair. Perhaps, if I wrote to her, it might help.

If I had been at home, I wouldn't have bought my wine in Colquhoun's, and I wouldn't have played golf with Bill Tulloch.

Mrs Borthwick, good luck. I hope McCann is a good father to Lenore.

Susan, I have a premonition about you. When I come back, you will not be among those left.

As for you, Helen, I'm glad you gave Henry his wishes, the piper and the Union Jack. I might even have worn my medals at the graveside, in his honour. I don't think I would have been showing off.

16

When I got back to Linda's, I found that, thanks to Morland, very comfortable quarters had been got ready for me, a big upstairs bedroom with bathroom attached, and with a magnificent view of the hills and the distant Pacific. At my window, bougainvillea grew, attracting bees, birds, and butterflies. The air inside and out was fragrant. Once I was settled in, there were the grounds to explore. I said good evening to Apollo, clutching his lyre. Being of bronze, he did not answer. I exchanged a few words with one of the guards. They had a hut of their own among the trees. Before dinner, I sat on the terrace drinking chilled white wine. Now and then Morland appeared, smiled, and asked if there was anything I wanted.

There was something I wanted very much: the company of my hostess. I hadn't seen Linda since breakfast. As a guest, I could hardly ask the servants questions about their mistress. I wanted to tell Linda about poor Millie, Henry and his piper, and Hector dead among his cats.

At last, after a solitary though excellent dinner, during which I had drunk a bottle of wine, I spoke to Morland on the terrace, where I was drinking brandy.

'Is Mrs Birkenberger at home?' I asked.

It had occurred to me she might have gone visiting. Now and then, I thought I had heard cars coming and going.

'Yes, she is at home,' replied Morland.

'She's not ill, is she?'

'No.'

'I was supposed to be helping her with her memoirs.'

'Yes, she told me.'

'Has she changed her mind? Does she now want me to leave?'

'I don't think so.'

'Do *you* still think I should?'

She hesitated. 'Perhaps it would be better.'

'Right. I'll leave in the morning. I don't want to stay where I'm not wanted.'

Morland went off, saying she would let Miguel know he was to drive me to my daughter's in the morning.

I kept on drinking and the more I drank, the sorrier I was for myself, and more resentful. It was callous and arrogant of Linda to invite me to stay and then ignore me. I was a Scotsman, member of a proud nation. I wasn't going to let myself be treated contemptuously.

The upshot was I got up and staggered off in search of Linda, to demand an explanation and an apology.

I didn't knock on her door, because, as I told myself, I wasn't a stranger who needed to knock. I was a guest who had been to bed with my hostess. That I had been Casaubon at the time and she Dorothea was immaterial.

The door wasn't locked, for everybody in the house, including me, knew that no one was allowed to disturb her.

The room was lit by a wall lamp with a pink bulb. In the big bed some activity was going on. The first thing I made out was not Linda's face but her bottom, rising up and down, pinkly, in what, if she had been alone, would have been strenuous exercise. The next thing I saw was a pair of feet, placed well apart, with the toes upwards, so they couldn't be hers. Besides, they were big and strong, evidently belonging to a man much younger than me.

So the dirty rumour was true, about Linda hiring young studs.

Despite my befuddlement, I felt, to begin with, not horror or jealousy or disgust, but pity. I wanted to go over and tell her that, if she sought oblivion, she had every right to choose any way she wished, in her own house, though I would have had to point out that this particular way would only be effective for the short time it lasted.

I felt affection as well as pity. I remembered the man in the library. He was very poor, and an outcast. Linda was very rich but she was an outcast too.

Though she did not see me, she realised there was an intruder in the room. She screamed obscenities in Spanish.

Back in my own room I locked the door and sat down, shaking all over. I was doomed. I had disturbed the monster in her lair.

But that was nonsense. Linda wasn't a monster. She was just an old woman who liked and needed sex. If she had been an old man hiring starlets, she might have been sniggered at but no one would have called her a monster. Most people, certainly most men, would say that it was her business, good luck to her, provided it was done in private.

I had invaded her privacy. If she had been a Chinese empress, she would have had my tongue cut out. Being a rich old lady with influence at the Country Club, she might get my temporary membership withdrawn.

Before going to bed, I packed my suitcases in readiness for a quick getaway in the morning.

I had meant to get up very early but I had had a very troubled sleep, so that it was nearly nine when I awoke. Quickly I showered, shaved, and dressed.

I was about to leave the room when there was a knock on the door.

It was Morland.

'Mrs Birkenberger is having breakfast and invites you to join her.'

I could only gape.

'Shall I tell her you'll be with her shortly?'

149

I nodded.

Had last night really happened, or had I dreamt it? Certainly my headache was evidence that I had drunk far too much.

My legs were still shaky when I made for the terrace.

In a white morning coat Linda was like any other elderly rich woman whose only worry was the putting on of weight.

'Going somewhere?' she asked with a smile.

She was referring to my Lunderston Golf Club blazer.

'I was thinking of visiting my daughter,' I mumbled.

'Sit down and have some breakfast.'

I sat down. I didn't have much of an appetite.

'Did you drink too much last night?' she asked sympathetically.

'I'm afraid so.'

Bravely I helped myself to toast and marmalade.

'Do you mind if I ask you a few rather personal questions, Professor?'

I cursed my headache. If the questions were too personal, I would need a clear head to parry them.

'Not at all,' I said. 'Ask away.'

If I had to lie to her, I would without compunction. She had no right to pry.

'You told me your wife's father was a doctor, but you didn't say what your own was.'

My lies were ready. They always were.

'He was a solicitor. What Americans call a lawyer.'

'He can't be still alive.'

'No. He was killed in the war.'

'That would be the First World War?'

'Yes.'

'He must have been quite young.'

'He was twenty-nine.'

'What age were you then?'

'Eight.'

'Were you an only child?'

'Yes.'

'Your mother would have been an educated woman?'

'Yes.'

'Did she have to work after your father's death?'

Mixing truth with falsehoods wasn't easy, especially with a severe headache and also, to be fair to myself, with a cancerous conscience.

'Yes. As a schoolteacher.'

'So you grew up and went to college and became a schoolteacher yourself?'

'Yes. I wanted to be a lawyer but we couldn't afford it.'

'You'd have made a good one. You've got a smooth tongue.'

What did she mean by that?

'Were you in the war?'

I could safely tell the truth here. 'Yes. North Africa. Four years. Royal Corps of Signals. Sergeant.'

'Just a sergeant? Not an officer?'

'Just a sergeant. I was very young.'

'Did you win any medals?'

She was being ironic. I answered plainly. 'Yes, I did. The Military Medal.'

'Was that the kind everybody in uniform got?'

'No. It was more special than that.'

'Was it given for bravery?'

'That's what they said.'

'So you were a hero?'

'I wouldn't say that.'

'There's more than one kind of bravery, isn't there?'

What was she getting at?

'When did your mother die?'

'When I was in North Africa.'

'Did you get to her funeral?'

'No.'

'But they told you where she was buried?'

'Yes. I often visit her grave.'

That was my worst lie yet. I hadn't visited that cemetery in the past 30 years. I wouldn't know how to find the grave. There was no headstone.

'I don't know where my mother is buried,' said Linda.

I took out of my pocket-book the snapshot of Susan Cramond's mansion in Goatfell Avenue. I handed it to Linda.

'Where I was born,' I murmured.

'Very big, very impressive, Professor. Do you still live there?'

'I'm afraid not. It had to be sold.'

'Where do you live now?'

'In what we call a bungalow; much humbler.'

Her smile was friendly, but there was something else in it. Was it scepticism?

'If you would like to meet me in what I call my study at eleven o'clock, it'll be my turn to tell the truth. Can you put off your visit to your daughter?'

'Yes, of course.'

In Linda's study, or private sitting-room, what struck me most was a crucifix on the wall, made of wood and crudely executed. It seemed out of place among all those artistic expensive ornaments.

'It was my mother's,' said Linda.

She was wearing a demure black dress. Adding to the nunlike effect was the absence of make-up and jewellery. Her hair had been arranged without artifice.

On a table was a pile of notebooks with black covers.

'Your manuscript?' I asked.

'Handwritten. If you have trouble making it out, just ask. But first I'd like to talk. It's easy to tell lies if you're writing them down in private. It's not so easy when you're speaking face to face. Don't you agree, Professor?'

152

'Yes.'

'I'm going to say things that I've never said before, to anyone.'

'I'm honoured, Linda.'

'As far as I know, I was born seventy years ago. There's no certificate to prove it. Where I lived, we didn't bother with things like birth certificates. It was a one-room shack made mostly of tarry paper, among other shacks like it. This was on the outskirts of a small town north of San Francisco. Today all the shacks have been cleared away. Expensive flats and nice gardens have taken their place. We were mostly Mexicans: field workers; dirt-poor. Some of the old people remembered that the whole of California had once belonged to us and, when they had drunk too much tequila, they sang songs about it. I remember those songs.

'I never knew my father. He took off months before I was born and never came back. My mother hardly ever spoke of him, not because she was bitter about him deserting her but because she was ashamed. She thought that, if she had been a better wife, he wouldn't have left. If she had been a better-off wife, he wouldn't have. I guess he just got sick and tired of being poor and went off to make his fortune. We never heard of him again. Likely he drank himself to death in some crummy lodging-house. He was half-Irish and half-Mexican. He said his name was O'Brien. I was christened Carmelita O'Brien.

'My mother was Mexican, though she used to say she had some Blackfoot blood in her. She had more pride and dignity than anybody I ever knew, and I've met Presidents and their wives. There were times when she had to whore to feed me and my sister. There was no welfare in those days. People starved.

'Are you shocked, Professor?'

I was. 'Do you really want to make these things public?' I asked. 'They are your business, no one else's.'

'I want everybody to know. They say that it's the poor who help the poor. It was the case with us. Not many people can enjoy themselves so much with so little as Mexicans. In Mexico you can come at night to a town that seems deserted. You drive through streets with the houses dark and silent. You begin to think a plague must have struck the place and the people are all dead in their houses. Then suddenly you come to a big open space, the *plaza mayor*, the *zocalo*, and it's lit up, the people are sitting at tables drinking beer or tequila, there's music, and there's not a gloomy face to be seen. You know that here are people who've learned that happiness is to be found in one another's company and being poor can't stop that.

'There are Americans here in California, you'll find lots of them at the Country Club, who despise Mexicans and think they're dirty, dishonest, and stupid. They judge the country by towns like Tijuana and Mexicali. They've never seen Taxco and Guanajuato.'

'I would like to visit those towns some day.'

She smiled. 'Maybe we'll go together. I've said my mother was the most dignified woman I've ever known. In this house there are johns fit for a President or a King, works of art, decorated with painted flowers, smelling sweetly. You've seen them, you've used them. Did you look dignified? I guess not. But my mother did, on that stinking rusty can with weeds growing out of the ground at her feet. I hated to go. I put it off to the very last minute and then there was usually someone in. Yet there my mother would sit like a queen. She never complained. That was what gave her her dignity. She never complained. Have you noticed how people who complain, whether with good cause or not, can't help sounding and looking selfish and mean? Me, I'm still dissatisfied, as you've noticed, and yet there's nothing I can't afford if I want it. My mother had nothing but me and my sister and yet you'd have thought she had everything. Sometimes I got mad at her, for I thought she should have been complaining like hell. Of course I was very young and didn't realise how much she must have been suffering. I told you I like to sleep alone. Once, when I was about six, I woke up and found in the bed beside me a customer getting his dollar's worth out of my mother. Would you like to see her?'

She handed me a small photograph, worn at the edges with much handling.

This small black-haired thin-faced woman could have been anyone's mother 60 years ago, she looked so ordinary. She could have been my own. The dignity of self-sacrifice was certainly there. So too, inevitably, was a certain coarseness, for who that had worked long hours in fields, entertained whoremongers, and pissed into a rusty can, could look refined?

'Here's one of me and Margarita. I was eight then. She was ten. She died two years later.'

Was that the shithouse in the background? They were holding hands. Linda, the smaller, was biting her lip to keep from laughing. Even then she looked indomitable. She had come a long way. Few journeys had been more remarkable.

Her book could have greatness in it.

'They say I was good-looking, but I was plain compared to her.'

Yes, the older girl was beautiful, but too pale, too delicate, too obviously marked for early death.

'There was work then, in the fields, hard work. It didn't harm me but it killed her. I saw her cough up blood. I don't know if doctors could have saved her but we couldn't afford them. So she died. I watched it happen. I couldn't believe it. I can hardly believe it even now. My mother broke her heart but her consolation was that it was God's will and Margarita was now safe in heaven. That was no consolation to me. I blamed God. I lost my faith then and I've never got it back.'

I glanced at the crucifix.

'That's to remind me of my mother, not of God.'

She smiled. 'Have you heard enough, Professor?'

'No, no. Please go on.'

'I remember the funeral as if it was yesterday. I didn't want to go. I didn't want ever to enter a church again. It must have been a comic sight, that funeral.'

'Comic? Why comic?'

'There was no coffin. We couldn't afford one. Just a sheet of cheap cloth. All those ragged half-starved mourners. The priest yawning and picking his nose.'

She didn't shed tears, just as she hadn't shed them then. She was heroic.

'When there were only two of us, there was no work. We often went hungry. We wore rags. Then my mother was lucky to get a job keeping house for an old guy who owned a general store. She had to sleep with him; that was part of the deal. The time came when he wanted me too in his bed. I was fifteen, well-shaped, and still a virgin. My mother said she'd cut my throat first. I said I'd cut his. One day I stole some of his money, about fifty dollars, and lit out for San Francisco without telling her. I meant to keep in touch but in those days I couldn't read or write, so I'd to do it by phone. My calls got fewer and fewer. Then one day when I phoned, the old guy told me he had fired her and he didn't know or care where she had gone. I didn't go back to look for her. It wasn't convenient. I was always going to, but it was never convenient. To be truthful, I was leading a kind of life she would have been ashamed of.

I guess I must have figured that I stood a better chance of making it without her. She had too many scruples. Does that make you laugh? A woman like her having scruples! What she did she did for me and my sister. What I did, what I've always done, was for myself. Selfish as hell, that was me then and it's still me now. Take warning, Professor. If I give a million dollars to help the poor I'm still being selfish. I'm hoping that my mother in heaven will forgive me, though I don't believe in heaven.'

But, having been brought up a Catholic, she must believe in hell; the priests would have made sure of that. She must think

156

that its worst tortures were in store for her. Her mother's intercessions would not save her.

'Well, Professor, that's enough for now. Do you still want to read what I've written?'

'Very much so, Linda. You don't seem to know what a marvellous triumph you have had.'

'Triumph? What do you mean?'

'Look at this house. Think of those paintings. You're honoured by millions.'

'I don't feel triumphant.'

But at dinner that night she was cheerful and, in bed afterwards, was understanding and sympathetic when, in my own private little hell, I failed to perform. She would have to send for Mr Casaubon, she said.

17

I was glad to take time off from editing Linda's memoirs, a slow task because her handwriting wasn't easy to decipher and also because much of the material was uncongenial to a closet Calvinist like me. I wanted to answer Helen Sneddon's letter. To the others, including Jean, I would send Christmas cards. I would send one to Chrissie Carruthers, though I was sure she wouldn't send me one.

Dear Helen

First let me say how sorry I was to hear about Henry. I used to tease him, but I was fond of him. I wish I had been there to help you endure his loss. But you have your family and your memories to sustain you.

Probably it's raining as you read this or snowing, and icy cold, with even the sparrows disconsolate and silent. Therefore, I hesitate to tell you that I'm writing on a sunlit terrace bright with flowers. Close enough to reach out and touch is a hummingbird sucking nectar from bird-of-paradise flowers. No, I am not in Madge's garden. Hers is not quite so grand. I am a guest of Mrs Birkenberger, who, you will remember, as Linda Blossom, was one of the most famous film stars of our time. Like ourselves, she is now old but has resisted the ravages of time better than most. No doubt her immense wealth has helped. I met her briefly during my last visit and we got on well. We've met again and she's invited me to help prepare her memoirs for publication. (I shall say something later about those memoirs.) For that purpose I'm staying in her house about 15 miles out of San Diego. An Elysian place. She owns a number of valuable paintings, including one I particularly like, by Rembrandt, an ironical self-portrait in his old age. I like to go and exchange looks with him. Conceit and falseness drain out of me. Come to think of it, Helen, you have the same effect.

I don't know what to say about Millie. I wouldn't be surprised if, when she comes out of her silence, she wants to go back to Tulloch. Her love for him, she will think, though soiled and broken, is still better than anything else in the world. But I doubt if he will want her back.

So Hector Liddell's dead. Did you know he was leaving his house to cats? His will probably have to be put down. He never liked me. You, and others who understood me, haven't minded what you called my showing off, but he hated me for it. He blamed me for Dresden, Hiroshima, and the concentration camps. He told me once that he believed in spiritual force, like Christ, whereas I believed in physical force, like Attila the Hun. But what spiritual force had he, poor man? Even his cats wouldn't listen to him.

He was convinced the human race would destroy itself. The prospect didn't displease him. I gather you have a similar fear. So do many others. Yet, if we do survive, I can imagine historians in 200 years being amazed at how trivial were the causes of dissension in the 20th century. That is to say, if humanity has grown up by then, which I doubt. It has always been my belief that, clever though we are, able to build cathedrals and invent atomic bombs, we are still, in our fundamental instincts, childish. Give a child of three a toy aeroplane and what does he do? He pretends that it's dropping bombs.

I hope I won't offend you, Helen, if I maintain that human beings are never more childish than in matters of religion. They believe what they want to believe, as children do. They create the kind of God that suits them, as children do. They believe that, if they're good, they get rewards but, if they're naughty, they get punished. For centuries they've shrieked at one another like children in a playground, 'Our God's better than your God', and they've killed millions to prove it. Take my daughter Madge and her husband Frank. Recently they gave themselves to Jesus, but they made sure it was a Jesus who hated Communists, distrusted blacks, and worshipped money.

I'm sorry, Helen. I didn't intend this letter to be so pessimistic. About two weeks ago, in the Public Library, I came upon an old man exuding the most horrible smell. God knows what caused it. Some dreadful disease, perhaps. He was ordered to leave. I didn't open my mouth to speak up for him. Like the rest, I watched in shamed silence. Perhaps he's dead now, for he looked as if he was dying, but, if to help him seemed impossible with him there in front of us, what hope have we of helping the millions we don't see? We write out our cheques for Oxfam and feel we have done all we can.

Just like me, Hector would have said, to whimper that I'm appalled by all the misery in the world and yet here I am living in the lap of luxury, like the only guest in a five-star hotel. The truth is, let me whisper it, I might be Linda's sixth husband. It is not beyond the bounds of possibility.

I mentioned earlier that I was helping her to edit her memoirs. Confessions would be a more accurate word. As her adviser, I have a problem. She is determined to tell the whole truth about herself, which means, alas, some shocking disclosures. She reveals, for instance, that her mother was a prostitute and that she herself when very young acted

161

in pornographic movies. I have hinted several times that such things should be kept secret, but she just smiles and says she has to tell it all, to get rid of it, as it's been poisoning her soul for many years. She was born a Catholic, remember. She says that most people hide the truth about themselves; that's why the world is so dishonest.

Usually she spends Christmas at her villa in Acapulco, but this year she's spending it here so that she and I can work on her book. It's going to be quite an occasion. It seems several people have invited themselves. From something she said, I got the impression that they were coming to beg money from her. You may have heard of some of them. I suppose you could call them famous. Josh Bolton, the author, who wrote the best-seller *Blood on the Ground*; he's also famous for having so many wives. Raimondo Bliss, who starred in many movies with Linda; he was the great lover. Senator Hazelwood, who obstructs every move to improve the lot of the poor. Not long ago he was accused of being mixed up in some shady financial dealings. I think he's heavily in debt and hopes Linda will help him out.

It should be an interesting gathering, don't you think? My daughter Madge, her husband Frank, and their two children Frank Junior and Midge have been invited for Christmas dinner. Madge doesn't quite approve of my friendship with Mrs B. but the other three are enthusiastic. Frank hopes to get promotion at his bank through Mrs B. and Frank Junior and Midge are thrilled at the chance of meeting the famous Linda Blossom, whose films at the moment are enjoying a revival among the intelligentsia.

Presents will be exchanged. What present could I give to a woman who has everything? Something of little monetary value but of great value in human terms. What, though? Then it occurred to me. Why not my Military

162

Medal? I brought it here to show to my grandchildren but I haven't done so yet because, as a consequence of the Vietnam War, they profess contempt for war and all its manifestations. Older Americans are the very opposite. They revere medals. So I thought, why not present Linda with mine. I shall hang it on the Christmas tree, with the other baubles.

Please write again, Helen. I amaze myself with a hunger for news of home. I used to tease Kate because of the thoroughness with which she read the *Lunderston Gazette*, every advertisement and, if the school sports prizewinners were given, every name.

It's a great sadness to me that you, Henry, and I are never going to be able to celebrate another Hogmanay together. Would I were with you both to hear the bells of Lunderston peal out the old year and ring in the new, and share a cup of kindness. I used to say – you smiled tolerantly – that I didn't care where I died or where I was buried but, at this great distance from home, in this alien sunshine, I find I like the idea of being laid to rest beside Kate in the cold glaur of St Cuthbert's kirkyard, on a grey day, with clouds obscuring the Sleeping Warrior.

I grieve with you, Helen. I hope that I am proved wrong and you and Henry meet again.

With my very best wishes.

I handed the letter to Morland to be posted.

She glanced at the address. 'Is this your home town, Mr McLeod?'

'Yes. A beautiful little place on the Firth of Clyde, where everybody knows everybody and we all wish one another well.'

An absurd exaggeration, of course, but that was how I felt then.

'Would you not be happier there at Christmastime, among your friends?'

163

Again that sibylline quality was in her voice and in her eyes.

'I hope I have friends here,' I said.

'Among people you can trust,' she added.

I was taken aback . . . Who here did she think was not to be trusted? She could mean only Linda.

She knew Linda better than anyone. She was in Linda's confidence. What did she know that she could not tell me?

'I'm looking forward to spending Christmas here,' I said.

'Good luck then,' she said, with a smile of goodwill that somehow caused me more foreboding than her sinister smile a minute ago. Was she quite right in the head?

A few days ago, unable to sleep, I had gone out about midnight for a stroll in the grounds in the moonlight. Hearing a splash, I had walked towards the swimming pool. In it was Morland. The moonlight had glittered on her breasts.

From behind a bush I had watched. Up and down the pool she had swum slowly, now doing the breaststroke, now on her back. When at last she climbed out, I saw that she was quite naked. She did not immediately dry herself or wrap herself in a towel. She stood looking up at the moon, stretching out her arms to it, like, I thought, a goddess of antiquity under a curse: such a one as Ulysses might have encountered during his journey home. Here she was begging to be relieved from it. I remembered that she had once killed a man.

Perhaps she did have the gift of foresight. Perhaps I should heed her warnings. But it was too late now.

PART THREE

1

To oblige Linda, I offered to go with Miguel in the Cadillac to fetch Bolton and his wife from the airport.

Linda spoke affectionately about him.

'Josh looks more like an all-in wrestler than a writer, with thick ears and a broken nose, but bear in mind, Professor, he didn't have your advantages. He wasn't born in a big house in its own grounds but in a walk-up apartment in the Bronx, with garbage in the streets and winos in the lobbies. His father wasn't a lawyer but a Jewish tailor, who as often as not was out of work. Not all Jews are rich, you know. There was little money in the house. Josh's mother was an invalid. He had to be tough to survive, so it isn't any wonder that he hasn't got your polite manners and classy looks. I'm telling you because I don't want you making the mistake of looking down your nose at him. If you did, you might get a bloody lip. Just remember, Professor, you didn't write one of the best books about the war. Josh did. I was surprised when you said you didn't like it. It's got lots of cuss words, I admit, but you were a soldier yourself, so you know soldiers fuck and cunt in every sentence. According to Josh, they did it in King Aldred's day too. When King Alfred burnt the cakes he didn't just say, 'How careless of me', he probably said, 'For fuck's sake!' But maybe it was the sex in the book that put you off. You're a bit of a Scotch prude, aren't you? That gives you a peculiar attitude to sex. You think it should be done in a gentlemanly way. In Josh's book it's done with sweat and grunts and groans and curses. That's more natural, isn't it?'

167

I couldn't resist a little irony. 'Don't animals do it in silence and with grace? Even elephants.'

Linda laughed, quite heartily. 'I've never seen elephants do it but you could be right. I wondered where you got your own method. Now I know. But Josh lives the truth in his life. It gets him into trouble. He was once jailed for giving a black eye to one of the bitches he married. She was spending all his money and was cheating on him behind his back, so wasn't it a truthful act on Josh's part to give her a black eye? It didn't hold him back that the other guy was a heavyweight boxer. Josh had a go at him too and ended up in hospital, with a broken nose and two black eyes. Now a gentleman like you, Professor, would be courteous to a woman cheating on you but you would have hated her guts. When Josh got out of jail, he threw a party for her and invited the boxer. It led to another punch-up but that wasn't Josh's fault. People just happen to behave naturally when he's around. I think that helps to make him a good writer. If you're wondering if I ever went to bed with him, the answer's no. It nearly happened once, but his socks were smelly. I bet you change your socks every day, Professor.'

'Every second day, Linda. We Scots are economical as well as prudish.'

'I'm looking forward to seeing you and Josh together.'

'What age is he?'

'About sixty-five, I would say.'

'How many times has he been married?'

'One less than me. Four times. The difference was I got alimony, he had to pay it. That's why I'm rich and he's poor.'

'Have you met his present wife?'

'No, I haven't. I've heard her father was a Governor some- where. I've also heard she's as ugly as sin. Josh has always had a weakness for upper-class dames. I expect because, like me, he's so low-class himself. You and Annabel should get on well, Pro- fessor.'

'Has she money of her own?'

'Are you kidding? Do you think she'd have married Josh if she'd had money? She's helped him to spend all his. He's grudged her nothing. Is that love, Professor?'

'A kind of love anyway.'

She smiled. 'How many kinds are there?'

'Dozens.'

'They're coming here to borrow money,' she said. 'No. Borrowing means having the intent of paying back. Neither of them has that intention. It's a Christmas gift they're looking for. The same goes for my other guests. They're all in deep trouble financially and they want me to buy them out of it.'

'May I ask how much Mr Bolton is hoping to borrow?'

'One hundred grand was the sum he mentioned, but he'd take more.'

'Good God! May I also ask if you intend to give it to him?'

'That's my business.' Then she gave me a funny look. 'But it could be your business too.'

'In what way?'

'Wait and see.'

'These other guests, Linda. Why are you letting Senator Hazelwood come? Isn't he notorious for his reactionary views? He would abolish welfare and food stamps if he could.'

'I know Leonard personally. My fourth husband was a politician. He was a reactionary too.'

'Yet you married him?'

'He was rich, very rich.'

'You disappoint me, Linda.'

'You disappoint me, Professor. I knew what I was doing. What I got out of him I gave to the poor; at least half a million.'

'I see.'

'No, you don't. You can't. We're talking about millions of dollars. It's a different ball game.'

'Yes, I understand that. But why Senator Hazelwood? Many people think he's a crook.'

'I think he's a crook.'

'Why didn't you tell him that he wouldn't be welcome?'

'But, Professor, he's a friend of the President. He's a Senator, with a lot of influence. Also, there's his wife Solace.'

'Solace?'

'That's her name. A Southern lady. Her great-grandfather was a Confederate general. Her family home had eight columns at the front door. In the past they owned dozens of slaves. She drinks like a fish. Her father blew his brains out. You'll enjoy meeting her, Professor. She calls black people niggers, to their faces.'

'Why do you think I'll enjoy meeting a woman who's a racist and a drunkard?'

'She says what she thinks. Isn't that admirable?'

'It isn't, if what she says is obnoxious.'

'I don't know about obnoxious, but it's never dull when Solace is around. She insults everybody. She once insulted the President. She'll insult you, Professor.'

'And yet they're coming to borrow money? I'd have thought they would have been humble.'

Linda laughed. 'Humble? Solace humble? Never in a million years. Leonard's not going to borrow money. He wants me to invest in some deal that, he says, will double my money in a couple of years.'

'Is it legal, this deal?'

'Knowing Leonard, I don't suppose it is, not altogether. Do you think I should give him the money? Two million dollars was the sum he mentioned.'

'As you said, Linda, this is a different ball game, one I'm not eligible to play. I don't even know the rules. But surely you have financial advisers?'

'Dozens. Including your son-in-law, who works in the bank.'

Was this my chance to speak up for Frank?

'I think Frank's advice would be sound, Linda.'

'I guess it would. We'll talk about it later. I want you to tell me what you think about my book. Is it any good?'

'I haven't finished it yet, Linda. Your handwriting isn't easy to read. But I'm finding it interesting, honest, and serious.'

'As serious as *Middlemarch*?'

'Yours is a very different kind of book, Linda.'

'I'll say!'

'I've marked some passages I'd like to discuss with you.'

'You think I should leave them out?'

'Or tone them down. They could be regarded as libellous.'

'But they're all true.'

'You don't have to reveal things just because they're true. You're entitled to keep them to yourself.'

'That's where you and I disagree, Professor. What do they say in court? The truth, the whole truth, and nothing but the truth.'

'But you're not on trial, Linda.'

'All the time I was writing it, I felt I was on trial. So I had to tell the truth. You know, Professor, all my life I've been looking for someone to tell me the truth.'

There it was again, that absurd, aggressive obsession with the truth.

'The truth about what?' I asked.

'About everything.'

'That's a very tall order, Linda.'

'Do you see yourself in the part, Professor?'

It was my turn to laugh. I didn't do it very convincingly.

'Do *you* see me in the party?' I asked

'I'm not sure. I haven't made up my mind yet. Have you told me the truth about yourself?'

'Linda, the hardest thing in the world is to tell the truth about oneself. No one's brave enough or rash enough. Not even you, my dear. Evasions, distortions, omissions, embellishments are inevitable. We're human beings, not gods. There are so many things we don't know, even about ourselves.'

She was amused. 'I like that "embellishments". But, Professor, it all sounds like excuses.'

She stood up. 'Time for bed. Thanks for the conversation, Professor. I like talking to you.'

'Why not call me Gregor?'

It would represent a step forward in intimacy and trust. She was not prepared to take it.

'Good night, Professor,' she said, and walked away.

When she was gone, I poured myself more brandy. Was she on to me? Should I hurry after her, remembering to knock this time, and confess?

No. She had just been guessing. No one could have told her, for no one knew, not even Madge. My lies were buried too deep. If I kept my nerve and went on practising Ulyssean guile, I could bring it off.

When I went to my own room, a bit unsteady on my feet, I took out of the drawer the small satin-lined box in which I kept my Military Medal. I pinned it to the lapel of my jacket. Looking at myself in the mirror, I reflected that wooing my hostess needed more nerve than sitting in a tent, tapping out signals with dead men lying at my feet.

2

Unlike most international airports, San Diego's is in the heart of the city. Planes skim downtown buildings as they come in to land. Passengers therefore look more relieved than usual at having landed safely. It was not, however, relief that I saw on Josh Bolton's battered face but adoration, as he kept looking up, for she was taller, at his wife. She was haughty, which I had expected, but also spectacularly ugly, which I had not, in spite of what Linda had said about her. I had attributed that to spiteful exaggeration. Her nose was so big and her chin so long as to be almost deformities. Yet she was dressed to attract attention, in a long loose white dress, big white hat, and white gloves up to her elbows. Bystanders gazed with wonder and derision at Bolton, not because they recognised him as the famous author who had taken part in so many literary and marital squabbles, but because of his rashness and fortitude in having taken as his wife or lover a dame so unlovely and yet so imperious, for whose sake too he had dressed ridiculously in a white suit, white hat, white shoes, and pink tie. It did not go well with his broken nose and cauliflower ears.

I went forward and introduced myself. 'How do you do? Gregor McLeod. Here on Mrs Birkenberger's behalf to welcome you to sunny California.'

Bolton gave me a hostile glance, which quickly turned into a good-natured grin. He held out a huge hand which had a grip like iron.

'Pleased to meet you, Gregor,' he said.

'Josh!' cried his lady.

He cringed. 'Sorry, Bel. Gregor, meet my wife, Bel.'

'My name, Mr McLeod, is Annabel.'

Her tone, though harsh, was friendly. After eyeing me up and down, she had decided that I would pass for a gentleman.

We waited at the entrance for Miguel to bring the car.

'Linda said you were a professor,' said Bolton. 'What university?'

Perhaps I ought to have confessed that it had been Linda who had conferred the professorship on me and not an academic council, but I did not. I decided I could get away with it. The Boltons, come to beg, were in no position to be inquisitive.

'Glasgow,' I replied. 'Emeritus, of course. I retired a few years ago.'

'You look distinguished enough to be a Harvard professor,' said Mrs Bolton. 'Doesn't he, Josh?'

'Sure does.'

'Glasgow University is much older than Harvard,' I said. 'It was founded in 1451, long before America was discovered.'

Irony was wasted on her, but not on Bolton.

'What faculty?' he asked.

'English Literature.'

'I expect you specialised.'

'Scottish medieval poets.'

'I'm afraid you've got me there, Professor.'

Which was why I had chosen them.

In the car, Mrs Bolton sat between us. Her haunch pressed into mine. She put her hand on my knee, not on his, to steady herself as we went round corners.

Bolton did not mind. Nothing she did or said could offend him. He was that much in love.

'How's Linda?' he asked.

Mrs Bolton stiffened at this mention of her hostess. She hated this errand to cadge money from a woman whom she considered her inferior in everything but wealth and beauty.

'In excellent health and spirits,' I replied.

'She mentioned on the telephone that you were helping her with her memoirs.'

'Writing them for her, she should have said,' said Mrs Bolton. 'She's uneducated and illiterate.'

'Not at all,' I said. 'All I'm doing is correcting the grammar and spelling and offering a suggestion or two. It will be Linda's book and no one else's.'

'I hear she's been offered an advance of half a million,' said Bolton, enviously.

'Unreadable trash, full of filthy Hollywood gossip,' said Mrs Bolton. 'Let's be honest. She may be our hostess, but she's vulgar and common. Is that not so, Mr McLeod?'

I did not answer.

'Considered once to be the most beautiful woman in the world,' said Bolton.

I was surprised at his tactlessness. Beauty should have been a subject for him to avoid. His wife at once took revenge.

'May I compliment you, Mr McLeod, on being in such good physical condition. Just look at Josh. That stomach. That red pudgy face. Those bags under his eyes. Too much drinking. Too much smoking, too little exercise. Those books he's written, with all that sex in them. You'd think he was a great performer himself. The truth is, he's incapable of making love. As our hostess would say, he just can't get it up.'

I expected Bolton with his infamous temper to slap her on the face and retort that, if she wasn't so fucking ugly, he'd have no trouble getting it up. He would have been justified. Instead, he looked at her with wistful forgiveness.

Since there was nothing pertinent for anyone to say after that, there was silence till the car arrived at the house.

Confronted by the evidence of Linda's great wealth and good taste, Mrs Bolton decided that, as someone come to beg, her best tactic would be friendliness, with a little condescension. Therefore, when Josh kissed their hostess, she followed suit but not so exuberantly, and conveyed that she just couldn't help being more gracious and ladylike.

I interpreted Linda's grim smile as meaning: the big cunt has a face that frightens babies and hasn't a cent to her name, so why the hell not put up with her, for Josh's sake?

At dinner that evening, Linda was wearing a red velvet dress so low at the neck that half her breasts were exposed. It was the one she had worn when acting as Lady Madeleine. Her jewellery was all diamonds. This was to outsparkle Mrs Bolton. Bolton, clownish in a blue tuxedo with glittering lapels, asked, rather shiftily, if she was expecting other guests. She replied, speaking like Lady Madeleine, 'Yes, Josh, four others. Including my old friend Raimundo Bliss.'

'I thought he was dead,' said Mrs Bolton.

'He is not in good health, I'm sorry to say.'

'Is he coming by himself? Doesn't he always have a young whore with him, pretending to be his granddaughter?'

'Since his health is not good, he has to be accompanied by a nurse.'

'Some nurse!' Mrs Bolton laughed.

She kept ignoring her husband's warning frowns.

'I hear the poor old guy's dying on his feet,' said Josh, sympathetically. 'Aids, I suppose.'

'With syphilis thrown in,' said Mrs Bolton.

'I think I mentioned he was my friend,' said Linda, grimly. 'He's coming here to borrow money. Like you, Josh.'

That shut Mrs Bolton up.

'Is the old guy in trouble?' asked Josh.

'He's in debt.'

'To loan sharks?'

'Yes.'

'Then he is in trouble.'

'They've threatened to make a mess of his face, and he's very proud of his face. It's still very handsome.'

'How much is he in for?'

'One hundred thousand dollars.'

'My God, a hundred grand. The old bugger must have made a packet in his day. Where's it all gone?'

'Look who's talking,' cried Mrs Bolton.

'Raimundo was always too generous for his own good,' said Linda.

'I saw him in a movie once,' said Mrs Bolton. 'He had to blow his brains out at the end. He should do it now for real. No one would miss him.'

'I would miss him,' said Linda.

'So you're going to help him out?' said Josh.

He couldn't help saying it glumly. If Linda helped Bliss out, she was less likely to help him.

'That's my business, Josh,' she said.

'Sure, of course it is. Who else is coming? Do I know them?'

'Senator Hazelwood and his wife Solace.'

Josh couldn't restrain himself. 'That reactionary bastard,' he cried. 'That slimy crook.'

'Josh!' snapped his wife, as if to a dog barking too loudly.

'But, Bel, just the other week he advocated the abolition of food stamps. He said hunger's the best way to drive a man to look for work.'

'Well, isn't it?'

'But what if there's no fucking work to be found? I beg your pardon, ladies.'

'There's always work to be found. Look at all the Mexicans who cross the border illegally. They find work.'

'Dirty low-paid jobs that no American wants. Frankly, Linda, I'm surprised you invited him.'

'I didn't. He invited himself. Like you, Josh. It seems he wants me to invest in some company that's bought land, in Missouri I think, and needs capital to dig out the phosphates or copper or whatever it is. He says if I put in a million, it would be trebled in a couple of years.'

'Sounds like the kind of crooked deal he'd be mixed up in,' said Josh. 'You've got advisers, Linda. I hope you consult them before you sign anything.'

'The Professor's my adviser.'

I laughed. I was sure she was joking. 'Your literary adviser, perhaps,' I said. 'I am not qualified to give financial advice.'

'But I'm asking you to advise me. What should I do about Raimundo? It's a moral matter too, isn't it? Should I give him the money to save him from the loan sharks?'

I felt like a boxer caught by an unexpected treacherous punch. I staggered mentally. I managed to whimper, 'Can't the law protect him?'

'Against the mob, the law's useless,' said Josh, cheerfully. 'Even if he was locked up in prison, he wouldn't be safe. Someone inside would get the message and unhappy Bliss would be found with his precious face smashed to pulp and his legs broken.'

'So the law's useless,' said Linda. 'What then, Solomon?'

I pretended not to notice the sneer.

'What he deserves,' said Mrs Bolton unwisely.

From Linda she got a smile of poisonous sweetness.

She was too stupid to be daunted. 'What's the use of paying his debts? He'd just get into more debt, wouldn't he?'

'Bel's right,' said Josh. 'And he'd be back with his begging bowl next Christmas. I know it's not up to me, but—'

'You're right, Josh,' said Linda. 'It's not up to you. It's up to the Professor.'

I began to think, with horror, that she was serious. 'Now, Linda, just a minute,' I cried.

'I'm saying this before witnesses, to show I mean it. If you say Raimundo should get the money, he'll get it. If you say he shouldn't, then he won't. And that goes for Josh too.'

178

Bolton and his wife looked at me in consternation, as well they might. They seemed convinced that Linda was in earnest. They thought that, to please and appease Linda, I would choose to save Bliss and let them go under.

I remembered my blundering into the monster's lair. I heard again in my imagination those desperate obscene screams. Was this her delayed revenge?

3

I was in my room, looking out at the moonlit garden and wondering if it had been this burden laid on me by Linda that Morland had warned me about, when there was a knock on the door. Foolishly, I thought it might be Morland come with a helpful suggestion.

It was Bolton, looking, in his absurd jacket, like a waiter in charge of room service in some five-star Las Vegas hotel, only it wasn't food and drink he was purveying but expensive unspeakable vice.

It was hard to see in this grey-haired pimpish fellow the audacious author who in his books had seized America by the scruff of the neck and made it look closely at its 'goddam polluted soul'.

'Could I have a word with you, Professor?' he muttered

'Certainly, Josh. Let's go down onto the terrace and have a smoke while we chat.'

'Whatever you say, Professor.'

The chairs on the terrace were comfortable. The air was balmy, fragrant, and moonlit. The Cuban cigars made the night still more delicious, as also did the cognac, the best France could provide.

It would be a great pity, I thought, to have to give all this up. Was Bliss worth it? Was Bolton? Come to think of it, Linda's giving to me the solemn responsibility of choosing could be interpreted as her putting me to a test, to find out if I was fit to be her sixth.

I felt more confident. I wasn't merely a guest talking to another guest. I was our hostess's favourite, with privileges denied others.

'Well, Josh, what was it you wanted to talk to me about?'

He puffed rather desperately at his cigar. 'You may remember, Professor, my article in the Lit. Review about fifteen years ago.'

'I don't know that I do, Josh.'

'Well, if you did, you'd remember the stink it raised in the academic world. Letters of protest from universities all over the globe – Oxford, Djakarta, Ulan Bator, Yale, you name it. Glasgow too, I shouldn't wonder. What I said in my article was that there was never any living writer worth a shit who owed anything to universities. I said they waited till you were safely dead and then they embalmed your stuff. I said they wouldn't touch anything that had blood, guts, and semen splashed over it. I said that what they liked were books stuffed with pseudo-mysticism, so that they could show how fucking smart they were, putting forward theories as to what the writers meant, though anyone with common sense knew that the writers meant fuck-all, they were just trying to be smart like them. In a word, I condemned academic mumbo-jumbo.'

I waved my cigar. 'You were entitled to your opinion, Josh. Honesty is all.'

'You're not sore then? You don't hold it against me?'

'Not a bit. Much is written but very little is worth reading.'

'That's very true. Mind you, Professor, I admit universities have their uses. Without them would we have nuclear bombs?'

I warmed to him for that irony. 'To be candid, Josh, I don't myself have a high opinion of universities. Some of the crassest remarks I've ever heard were made by the so-called experts of Academe. They write theses on abstruse subjects, of interest only to themselves and others like them, and are rewarded with doctorates. They then expect the rest of us to call them Doctor.'

'I couldn't agree more, Professor.'

'Call me Gregor.'

'Let me be candid too, Gregor. I owe you a personal apology. When I saw you at the airport, I thought, what a fucking old impostor, he's got all the makings of a high-class confidence trickster, he's got Linda thinking he's an aristocrat. She'll never see that he's after her money. That, Christ forgive me, is what I thought.'

'I can't speak for Christ, Josh, but I forgive you.'

'Thanks, Gregor. You're a real gentleman. I can see why Bel admires you.'

I laughed. 'Evidently a lady of great perspicacity.'

'I don't know about perspicacity, but she's got loads of class. Did I tell you her father was a Governor?'

'Linda mentioned it.'

'She was brought up in a Governor's mansion. She's met the people who matter.'

I remembered that Jean had used that phrase.

'May I amend that, Josh? The people who think they matter.'

'No, Gregor, the bastards do matter. They have the power to fuck up our lives and they do fuck them up. Hazelwood's a prime example. Tell me, Gregor, have you slept with Linda? Or should I say, knowing that the lady prefers to sleep alone, have you been to bed with her?'

'Now, Josh, you ought to know a gentleman never divulges such things.'

'Which means you have. Congratulations. Is it your design to marry her?'

'If Linda and I get married, it will be because we care for each other.'

'Sure. I get the message. I would say you're in with a good chance. I'll give you all the help I can. She's already asked me what I thought of you. I told her you could be the kind of guy she's been waiting for all her life.'

I didn't believe him. 'And what did she say?'

183

'She just smiled but she didn't contradict me. It wouldn't last long, your marriage. Linda likes changes, but you would be on to a good thing while it lasted, and it would be to Linda's benefit. We've got to make sure she doesn't waste a penny on that leprous old fucker Bliss.'

'Leprous?'

'Wait till you see him, especially when he's slobbering over a girl young enough to be his granddaughter.'

'But Linda likes him.'

'She pities him. She thinks she should be loyal to him, but she knows he's not worth it. Take my word, Gregor, she'll be relieved when you turn him down. She doesn't want to do it herself so she's handed the axe to you.'

'Yes, but I wish she hadn't. It's her money and her friend. It's really none of my business.'

'If you take my advice, you won't adopt that attitude. Linda likes to get her own way. If you want to get anywhere with her, do what she wants.'

I had to agree with that.

'Do you know why I'm here, Gregor?'

'Linda mentioned it.'

'There you are, you see. She takes you into her confidence. She trusts you. Gregor, I need that money. I've tried everywhere. No dice. If I don't get it, I'll lose Bel. It's as simple as that. It's as terrible as that. If I lost her, I wouldn't want to go on living.'

A whine had come into his voice.

'That's reckless talk, Josh,' I said, sternly. 'You've been married how many times?'

'Four.'

'So you've already lost three wives. Why should losing another drive you to despair? Have you any children?'

'Eight. All grown up.'

'Think of them, Josh.'

'They all hate Daddy's guts.'

184

'They may say so, but I'm sure in their hearts proper filial feelings exist.'

I knew I was beginning to sound pompous, but I couldn't help it.

'You're losing sight of the main issue, Gregor.'

'Not at all, Josh. What is the main issue? The disposal of one hundred thousand dollars. A goodly sum.'

'The lady's worth twenty million, forty if she sold those paintings.'

'I would never be a party to her selling them. Josh, in fairness to Linda, I must ask how you intend to pay her back.'

'Gregor, whether I intend to pay her back or not is no fucking business of yours.'

'I'm afraid it is, Josh.'

'Look, Gregor, I'll be honest with you. I know you're not loaded. What's a professor's pension? Chicken feed. How would ten per cent suit you? We're men of the world, Gregor. The lady need never know.'

'You're insulting me, Josh.'

'Twenty per cent then.'

'You've doubled the insult. No, Josh, before I can choose between you, I must talk to Bliss. That's only fair.'

'Would you, a Scotsman, a fellow countryman of John Knox, help to finance the corruption of young girls by a diseased old roué?'

'No, Josh, I would not. But I must judge for myself.'

I stood up, not too steadily.

He looked as if he would have liked to club me with the cognac bottle. I noticed that it was almost empty. It had been almost full when we had sat down.

He stood up too. He had something urgent to say.

Politely I waited and listened.

'What Bel said in the car wasn't exactly true but, just the same, I'd be obliged if you never mentioned it.'

It took me a few seconds to recall what she had said.

I patted him on the shoulder. 'Mum's the word, old man. Even if it is true, why repine? It would not be the end of the world.' Though, of course it would be if all men were similarly afflicted.

Chuckling at that brave jest, for after all I was myself only a four-out-of-ten man, I went off to my room, taking the long way, past the swimming pool. Alas, Morland of the splendid breasts was not in it.

4

Bliss arrived before lunch, having driven from Los Angeles in an open sports car painted shocking pink. Drab grey would have been more prudent, in that it would not have drawn attention to the driver, but I saw at once that, for Bliss, to be noticed, admired, and, above all, liked was as important to him as air or money. His hair was wavy, chestnut-brown, patently false. His cheeks were rouged, like a corpse's. Indeed he looked as if he had just passed through the hands of an artistic and conscientious mortician. 'Leprous' was not the word to describe him: it indicated life, however tainted. Cadaverous was more apt. His clothes contributed to the effect: a blazer of blue-and-white stripes, white silk shirt, blue cravat, white slacks, and blue shoes. Dressed thus, he would lie content in his satin-lined coffin. His perfume was a kind likely to be used by the most expensive embalmers. He had once been tall but now had a bad stoop. Even on that warm sunny morning, his hand was cold and clammy, and his voice amidst the birdsong was like a croak from the tomb. Destroyed by some cancer, he was ready for burial.

He was not alone. His companion, Amantha, could not have been older than 19. At first sight, she looked quite beautiful, with her big blue eyes and long fair hair that glittered like a model's in a shampoo advertisement. But her eyes were empty and she kept chewing gum, which increased the impression of inanity. An unbuttoned red blouse showed big fat breasts and knee-length yellow pants gave prominence to a bottom that reminded me of

Millie Tulloch's, except that Amantha's, as it were, was in full bloom while Millie's was past its best.

There were as many reasons for rejecting Bliss as there were hairs on the girl's head, and yet I found myself not liking the old reprobate and not having much pity for him either, but responding, reluctantly, to something in him, a childlike guilelessness, which had survived miraculously through a long life of tawdriness and self-indulgence.

All the same, as I watched him go off hand in hand with Amantha to their room, escorted by Linda herself, the Calvinist in me vowed, that if it was left to me, he would not get a cent.

Bolton saw my grimace of distaste. 'What did I tell you?' he said. 'Doesn't he turn your stomach?'

'He's loathsome,' said Mrs Bolton. 'Linda had no right to invite him when she's got other guests.'

'The poor fellow's ill,' I said cautiously.

'Putrescent,' said Bolton. 'He'll glow in the dark.'

'It's not funny, Josh,' said his wife. 'We know what he's got. Syphilis.' She enjoyed hissing the word.

'Backed up by Aids,' said Bolton cheerfully.

'He'll ruin that girl,' said Mrs Bolton. 'It shouldn't be allowed. He *deserves* to have his face smashed.'

She said those last words quietly, for Linda was coming back.

'Poor Raimundo,' said Linda, as she sat down. 'He won't last much longer.'

'What's wrong with him?' asked Mrs Bolton. 'Has he got some disease?'

'At least he'll die happy,' said Bolton.

Linda looked and sounded grim. 'What do you mean?'

'In Amantha's lovely arms.'

'She's his nurse,' said Linda.

'Isn't she too young for him?' asked Mrs Bolton.

'I wasn't any older when I married Al Birkenberger. Al was sixty-five. We were very happy.'

'But, Linda,' I said, 'you had more character in your pinkie than that poor girl has in her whole body.'

She glared at me. 'Is that so? I saw you getting a good eyeful of her whole body. If you fancy her sort, there are agencies that supply them. Just lift a telephone and one could be delivered in half an hour, like a pizza.'

Bolton tried to appease her. 'Anyway, good luck to the old guy. It's his business, not ours.'

'You can say that, Josh. The Professor can't.'

'Why can't I?'

'Because you're going to have to say whether or not Raimundo gets his loan.'

'Wasn't that a joke on your part?'

'It was no joke. I said it before witnesses. I meant it. I still do.'

'But, Linda, he's your friend and it's your money. Surely it's for you to say?'

'I've given it to you.'

'Be fair, Linda. You yourself called me a Scotch prude. To ask me to decide is unfair to Mr Bliss.'

'Why is it unfair?'

'Well, I have to confess that his association with that young girl does disgust me a little.'

'It disgusts everyone,' said Mrs Bolton.

'It doesn't disgust me,' said Linda. 'She's his nurse. She looks after him. What's disgusting about that?'

'Are they sharing the same room?'

'If he had a stroke – he's already had one – she wouldn't be much use if she was in another room.'

'Does Mr Bliss know?' I asked.

'That his life is in your hands?'

'Isn't that an exaggeration?'

'It's the truth. Yes, he knows. He's quite happy about it. He trusts you. He thinks you look *simpatico*.'

★   ★   ★

After lunch, Bliss came and sat beside me at the swimming pool. In Belsen he would not have been noticed, so gruesome was his emaciation.

He put his hand on my naked knee. I had to restrain myself not to strike it off.

'Do you mind if we have a little private chat?' he croaked.

Linda and the Boltons were seated a little way off, out of earshot. Amantha was on the other side of the pool. She had taken off the top of her bikini. She chewed gum and read one of the movie magazines she had brought with her.

'I believe Linda has entrusted you with a little commission,' he said with a giggle.

I said nothing.

'You know, Gregor, the last time I saw her she was full of self-doubt. Someone has given her back her confidence. We know who that someone is. Well done, Gregor. I'm not surprised, for you come from a country that has a reputation for putting moral value before financial gain.'

'I'm not sure such a reputation is justified. The Scots are as mercenary as other nations.'

'Was not Alexander Fleming, discoverer of penicillin and therefore one of the great benefactors of mankind, a Scots-man? He made little money out of his discovery. It's men like him who enable us to believe that people are fundamentally decent. You agree, don't you, that people are fundamentally decent?'

Inwardly I asked, 'What about murderous loan sharks? Or moribund old lechers?' I happened then to look across the pool. Amantha had put down her magazine and was rubbing more sun oil on her breasts. These glistened like balloons. In me, the disapproving grandfather wrestled with the dirty old man.

Bliss, damn him, read my mind. 'In all the literatures of the world,' he said, 'there are tales of old men being rejuvenated by comely young damsels.'

'Do the tales tell what the comely young damsels get out of it?'
I asked.

He giggled again. 'You'd be surprised. Amantha simply loves laving me from top to toe, as if I was her baby.'

'She does not look the maternal type, though well equipped.'

'Yes, hasn't she got gorgeous boobs? She suckles me. What exquisite joy.' There was a blob of slaver on his chin.

I felt like hurling him into the pool. Yet he had the knowing innocent look of the infant Christ in Renaissance paintings.

'If you like, Gregor, I'll send her along to your room tonight.'
Astonishment made me dense. 'What for?'

'She's so gentle and patient. She knows how brittle old limbs are. She will handle your member as if it was a flower.'

'No, thanks,' I said, somewhat inadequately.

'Linda wouldn't mind. Well, she ought not to but, just in case, we wouldn't tell her. After all, she's got her young studs. To be fair, if old men find rejuvenation in young women, why shouldn't old women find it in young men? High-born Roman matrons did it. Look at her. Isn't she marvellous for a woman her age? Rubens would have loved to paint her. He would have put her among his goddesses.'

In a green bikini Linda did look attractive for a woman of 70.

'She has had many lovers in her day. I was never one myself. Our relationship was more like that of brother and sister. In any case, I would never have had the courage. Do you know that she once almost castrated a lover? With her nails. A famous name. I won't say it. He must have said or done the wrong thing. It seems she dug in and wouldn't let go, like an angry cat. I discussed it at the time with a psychiatrist. He said that in the act of love some people because of inner tensions have orgasms of guilt not of joy. Linda has always been like that. Something to do with her childhood perhaps.'

I remembered the child of six waking up to find her mother being used as a prostitute.

'Even Al suffered, I believe, and she loved him.'

'Did you know Mr Birkenberger?'

'Very well. He produced many of my movies. You've seen the bust in the gallery? It's a good likeness. He was very generous. He left her millions and also those wonderful paintings.'

'He must have been an old man.'

'What's age? Some men are old at 20, others young at 80.'

He paused and again clutched my knee. 'To come to the point, when I mentioned to Linda that I was in need of a little loan to pay off some urgent debts, she said I'd to talk to you about it.'

'She shouldn't have. It's not my money.'

'But if you and she are to be married?'

'Are we? Did she say so?'

'Not in so many words, but, when she was speaking about you, there was something in her manner that intrigued me. She's never met anyone like you before. She seems to think you and she have a lot in common. I must confess I don't see it for, on the surface at any rate, you're very dissimilar.'

I knew what we had in common, but no one else did, not even Linda.

'I think the way you speak impresses her. Your accent suggests to us brash Americans dependability and probity. She told me you're helping her edit her memoirs.'

'Yes, I am.'

'Are they any good?'

'I think they're very good. She certainly tells the truth about herself. In fact, she is obsessed with telling the truth.'

'Oh dear. There could be some red faces then. May I ask if I feature in it?'

'You do.'

'Not discreditably, I hope.'

'She always speaks warmly of you.'

'Bless her. We go back a long way. In the old days there was prejudice against us Mexicans in the film world. We fought it together. You could bring dignity and security of mind to her in her old age. I already notice an improvement in her speech.'

Because she saw herself as Lady Madeleine.

'Shall we enter into a compact, Gregor? To help each other. You know of course what I am referring to? I need the money very badly. Shall I send Amantha to you tonight?'

'There is no need.'

'But I want to. I like to share with my friends.'

'Wouldn't Amantha object?'

'Object to doing a kindness? That is not in the dear girl's nature. Besides, she enjoys comforting old men.'

I grued, but managed to smile. 'The fact is,' I lied, 'I am to attend our hostess after dinner.'

'Ah. In that case, good luck. If you think you should need them, I have little purple pills. They have a side effect that I should warn you about. Sometimes their effect does not wear off for days, with, as you may imagine, inconvenient consequences.'

Later that evening he slipped into my pocket a small white box that rattled. It contained the purple pills. 'No more than two at a time,' he whispered. 'To be taken half an hour previously.'

I waited in my room for Linda to summon me. Confident that she would, for she had been affectionate during dinner, I swallowed two of the pills. The result, alas, was that I broke out in an itchy rash and remained quite detumescent.

It was as well that the summons never came.

5

The Hazelwoods arrived next day. Miguel was sent with the Cadillac to fetch them from the airport. No one went with him. Bliss, forever obliging, offered. He was sure to find the Senator repulsive, he said, but then, so would the Senator find him repulsive, which meant that they would keep a correct distance from each other. Linda said no.

They hadn't been told who their fellow guests were to be, so they hadn't had time to prepare themselves. Therefore, for that first minute we saw them plain.

The Senator gave me and the Boltons cold neutral stares, but Bliss he regarded with a repugnance astonishing in its virulence. What made it all the more shocking was that he was a handsome man of 60 or so, tall, tanned, and silver-haired. It was as if all the vicious prejudices in him had rushed to the surface at the sight of poor Raimundo.

His wife looked at all of us, including Linda, as if, as Bolton later described it, we were bags of shit. Her nose twitched, as if at a nasty stench. It was pudgy and red, that nose, an indication that, as Lunderston would have put it, she was fond of a bucket and it would take more than one bucket to get her paralytic. It was easy, though, to believe that she had once been a proud Southern beauty, that she had been born in a mansion with eight columns at the front door, and that, as Linda had reminded us, her father had blown his brains out in that same house.

Bliss, the absurd cheek-turner, offered his hand; it was contemptuously ignored. He asked politely if they had had a good flight from Washington, and again was shunned.

They showed no pity for Amantha, but she didn't notice. She had been told they had nothing to do with movies so, for her, they were nonentities.

Linda did not personally show them to their room. She left it to Morland.

'What a pair of obnoxious cunts,' said Bolton. 'Sorry, ladies, but that's what they are.'

'He's a buddy of the President's,' said Linda, 'and her Grand-daddy was a general in the Confederate Army.'

'No wonder they lost.'

'One cannot help feeling sorry for them,' said Bliss. 'How terrible to be so full of hate. How can they ever be happy?'

Mrs Bolton had no patience with such magnanimity. 'He looked at you, Mr Bliss, as if you were filth. If it was left to him, you'd be rotting in jail.'

'Instead of which I'm rotting out of it.'

'Raimundo never nears a grudge,' said Linda.

'Especially not at Christmas,' he said. 'But we shouldn't forget that her father shot himself when she was a child.'

'It was her who found the body,' said Linda.

'Did he know the gun was loaded?' asked Amantha.

'Have they any family?' asked Mrs Bolton.

'A daughter,' said Linda. 'She married a black.'

'I didn't know that. They've kept it very quiet.'

'He's a doctor. So is she. They run a clinic for the poor in Baton Rouge.'

'Linda helps to finance it,' said Bliss. 'It does wonderful work.'

'Have they any children?' asked Mrs Bolton eagerly. Evidently, she hoped they had, children who had taken after their father and so had black skins and thick lips.

Linda didn't have time to answer. Mrs Hazelwood was back

alone. Leonard, she said harshly, would not appear while Bliss was present. He was allergic to diseased trash.

We were all speechless, except Amantha, who remarked that she was allergic to raspberry-flavoured ice cream. It brought her out in itchy white spots.

Mrs Hazelwood waved Chung over and ordered a large gin and tonic. While waiting for it, she glowered at Bliss. 'Why don't you get the fuck out of here?' she said.

'To oblige you, lady,' he said, with a ghastly forgiving smile, 'I shall withdraw.'

'No, you won't,' cried Linda. 'Look here, Solace, if you're not going to treat Raimundo civilly, I'll have to ask *you* to withdraw.'

Mrs Hazelwood did not answer. She was too busy emptying the glass Chung had brought her. She was already thinking of her second, and her third.

Perhaps, too, in her fuddled mind she was remembering why she and her husband had come: to beg Linda to help them out of pecuniary difficulties.

It seemed to me she was at the same stage of desperation as her father had been when he had pulled the trigger. Those half-caste grandchildren were pistols at her head. She could end up mad.

That afternoon she came into the library looking for me. It was a wonder she was still able to walk, for at lunch she had emptied two bottles of wine. The Senator had had lunch in his room. She had heeded Linda's warning and left Bliss alone. She had picked on the Boltons instead, especially Annabel. 'Is it true you don't allow mirrors in your house, Mrs Bolton?'

I was reading when she came in. The book was Sir Walter Scott's *Old Mortality*. All of Scott's novels were there; all of Dickens's; all of Thackeray's; and all of George Eliot's. Every book sumptuously bound in red leather.

I stood up with a gentlemanly smile. Inwardly I cursed my luck. I should have stayed in my room, like the Boltons.

She put her hand on my arm, to help her stand upright.

Anyone looking in would have thought the blue-haired lady was propositioning the white-haired gentleman.

So she was, but what she was proposing was that I should go at once and tell our hostess she must get rid of Bliss and his little harlot.

I set her down in an armchair and myself sat on an adjacent sofa.

'Mrs Hazelwood,' I began.

'Call me Solace.'

'Solace, then. I shall be frank. I understand that your husband wishes Mrs Birkenberger to invest a large sum of money in a business enterprise. Let me assure you that he is going the wrong way about it by insulting Mr Bliss. Mr Bliss has been a friend of hers for many years. I need say no more.'

In fact, I needn't have said anything. She wasn't listening to me, she was staring into the past.

'When I was a young woman,' she said, 'I went out with the Klan once. We hung ourselves a nigger. He had molested a white woman. They said he had molested her but I didn't know whether he had or not. It made no difference. He screamed and pissed himself. He had on white pants. You could see he had pissed himself. We all laughed.'

Outside, workmen were erecting a large Christmas tree on the terrace. Their radio was blaring out seasonable music. I listened to 'Rudolph the Red-Nosed Reindeer' and saw in my imagination the black man dangling from the tree.

My blood turned to ice.

'It was the happiest time of my life,' she said.

All the evil of the world descended upon me then. Like a survivor of a nuclear holocaust, I did not know what to think or feel. There was no comfort in anyone's company. All that was good had come to an end.

The feeling lasted less than a minute but I would remember it all my life.

198

'That gorilla with his dream,' she said. 'I have a dream too. An America where all the blacks have been sent back to Africa and where white trash have been eliminated. Hitler had the right idea.'

What could I have said to that? What could anyone? Demosthenes would have been struck dumb.

Suddenly she realised where she was. 'Look at those books. Who reads them? Look at this house. Who owns it? A fat vulgar old tart. When I was young, you'd find her sort in their proper place, the brothels of Savannah. Do you approve of the world we live in, Professor, that rewards those who disgrace it, like that fat cow, and abuses those, like my husband, who try to elevate it?'

Did she really believe that about her husband? Yes, she did.

'How can a man of his stature be expected to beg from a creature like her?'

So that was it. It wasn't disgust at Bliss that was keeping the Senator in his room, it was a mixture of shame, anger, and maimed pride.

His wife's face then was the one under the pointed hood 40 or so years ago. The hanged Negro had come alive again and married her daughter.

To my great relief, she got up, muttering that she needed a drink, and staggered off in search of it.

6

When I told Linda that I was going to Madge's with the Christmas presents I had brought from Scotland and that I might spend the night there – after all it was Christmas Eve – she said she would be very disappointed if I wasn't present at dinner that night; she had a surprise arranged. In that case, I replied, I would certainly be present. I let myself wonder if the surprise might be a public announcement of our engagement. It would be like Linda to tell others before she told me.

Madge's family were all at home, though hardly in a state of Christmas amity and goodwill. Madge was quite cantankerous. When she was out of the room, Frank, in agitation, whispered the reason: she had resigned from the church, on the grounds that it was too mercenary. Unfortunately, she had been unnecessarily rude to Pastor Snodgrass. I took that to mean that she had carried out her threat and told the clerical buffoon to go kiss her arse. Well done, Madge, I thought, but you could have waited till after Christmas.

Frank Junior looked in, thanked me for my present, and went off again.

Midge did not appear.

'Are you going to stay the night, Dad?' asked Madge. 'It's Christmas Eve.'

'I'm afraid not, Madge. I promised Linda I would be back in time for dinner.'

'Oh, you did, did you? So you'd rather be with that bunch of strangers than with your own family? Of course, they're rich and important.'

'Mrs Birkenberger said she had a surprise for me. It could be that she's going to tell me that Frank's to have her account.'

'In that case, Dad,' cried Frank, 'you must go.'

I felt sorry for him and ashamed of myself.

'Have you talked to her about it?'

'Yes, Frank, I have.'

I hadn't, though. I was up to my ears in new lies. I had long ago been drowned in the old ones.

'I can't say I'm surprised,' said Madge. 'You've always wanted to associate with rich and important people.'

'If so, Madge, I never got much opportunity in Lunderston.'

'What opportunities there were you took. Look at the fuss when the Prince of Wales visited the golf club. Who played golf with him?'

'I was the golf-club captain at the time. It was my duty to play with him.'

'Then you made a point of being introduced to the Lord Lieutenant of the County, though you've always called yourself a socialist.'

'I was president of the Rotary Club at the time.'

'Wasn't it strange, you a socialist, being elected president by a bunch of Tory snobs? I never heard of you visiting the Old Men's Club. They were all poor pensioners there.'

That was regrettably true. I had always preferred the company of the well-off.

There was a reason but I was going to keep it to myself. Not even Kate had been told.

'Then there's that woman Cramond you're hoping to marry. She's rich, isn't she? She lives in a mansion.'

Frank was looking more and more puzzled. 'What's wrong with all that, honey?' he asked. 'Anyone would want to associate with successful people.'

She ignored him. 'I'm going to ask you straight to your face,

Dad. I'm not going to plead. I'm just going to ask. Will you stay and spend Christmas Eve with your family?'

I could have said they weren't acting like a family, but I didn't. It wouldn't have been the real reason for my preferring dinner at Linda's.

'Of course this house is a dump,' said Madge, 'compared to hers, and we're boring insignificant people compared to Mrs Birkenberger, and the Boltons, and the Hazelwoods.'

With that, she burst into tears and ran out of the room.

'It's not your fault, Dad,' said Frank. 'She's really pleased that you've made such important friends. It's Midge she's worried about.'

'But I thought Midge had admitted she's not pregnant.'

'Yes, but she still uses it as a threat. Would you like to talk to her, Dad? She respects you.'

'Does she?' I didn't believe it, but she was my granddaughter and, if I could, I should help.

'You'll have to knock hard on the door, Dad. She plays her music rather loud.'

'So I hear.'

The whole house now and then shook with the blast.

I took my present with me, a blue cashmere cardigan, made in Scotland.

Knocking on the door was no good, so I opened it and went in.

She was seated on the floor in a Buddhist posture. She was wearing a white shirt and very brief black briefs. She opened her eyes for a moment, saw it was me, and closed them again. She smirked like Buddha. She was trying to look wise and serene.

'Do you mind?' I roared, as I turned the knob that would produce blessed silence. But I didn't dare turn it off altogether. So some idiot continued to drool about love.

There was no chair, only a low pouffe, on which I had to sit as if on a chamber pot.

'I've brought you a present,' I said. 'It's a cardigan. It's blue. I hope you like it. Blue was your grandmother's favourite colour.'

She didn't open her eyes to look at it. 'Thanks. I've got nothing for you, Grandad. I've got nothing for anyone. Christmas shouldn't be commercial. Did Mom send you to snoop?'

'Your mother did nothing of the kind. She's very worried about you.'

It had often struck me that, while adults were frequently childish, the young were just as often repellently precocious.

'I bet she is. Tell me, Grandad, what, in your opinion, is the purpose of life?'

Man is never more thoughtful than upon the stool, Dean Swift had said but, on that low hard pouffe, I was in no humour to enter into a philosophical debate with my half-naked grand-daughter who was making her mother's life a misery.

'We've all got one thing in common,' she said, 'whether we're white or black or yellow or green or rich or poor or fat or thin or straight or queer.'

'And what is that?' I asked.

'None of us asked to be born.'

So what?, as she would have said herself.

'So we should show consideration for one another. Right?'

What bloody cheek, I thought.

'Who is it that shows the most consideration?'

Not teenage daughters, I felt like saying.

'I'll tell you. A mother looking after her baby. All that crap about the Madonna and Child, in all those famous paintings. Crap but true. It's the central symbol of our civilisation.'

Was this her way of telling me that, though she wasn't pregnant at present, she might well be so soon?

'A mother's obligation ends only with death. Right?'

I almost said, a father's too, but fathers were not so biologically obliged.

'So I ought to have a baby. Right?'

'Not in the near future, I hope.'

'Who the father is doesn't matter.'

Was this an apology for promiscuity?

'Maybe, in my case, it would be better if he was black. I would have to show it a lot more consideration than if it was white. I mean, with all the prejudice that's about.'

'Right.'

She grinned, opened her eyes, and changed the subject.

'Tell me about Linda Blossom,' she said. 'Do you sleep with her?'

'That's not a proper question for a girl to ask her grandfather.'

'I read in a magazine that she likes to sleep alone. But she's had dozens of lovers. Does a bell ring when it's time for them to get out of bed? Ha, ha. I'm looking forward to meeting old Raimundo Bliss. Do you think he'll make a pass at me? They say he likes them young.'

I hadn't mentioned Amantha.

'Frank Junior wants to meet Josh Bolton, the famous author. Dad wants to meet that unspeakable creep, Senator Hazelwood.'

I glanced at my watch. It was time to go. I stood up, with difficulty. 'Well, you'll meet them all tomorrow.'

'I'm looking forward to it. Mom says she's not going. But she'll go. She wants to see if Mrs Hazelwood is as terrible as they say. Is she?'

Yes, in the real sense of exciting terror. I shuddered. If Mrs Hazelwood was to go mad, let it not be tomorrow.

'If you're going, Grandad, would you please turn up the sound?'

'Don't you know listening to loud music causes deafness?'

'So what?'

I turned it up a little and left.

My legs were shaky. What if they went altogether? It had happened to men I knew. No more houghmagandy. Ha, ha, as Midge would say. No more golf.

Madge was back in the living-room. 'Well?' she asked. 'What's my daughter been saying to you?'

'We've been having a philosophical discussion.'

'Don't joke about it, Dad. Is she pregnant?'

'Not a bit, and has no intention of becoming so. I would say she sees pregnancy as a philosophical position, not a matter of morning sickness and much physical inconvenience.'

I couldn't resist glancing at my watch.

'You can't wait, can you, Dad, to get back to your rich friends. Because you look the part, you're keen to play the part.'

'And plays it very well,' said fatuous Frank.

'We're not taking her anything,' said Madge. 'It would be stupid. What could we give her? She's got everything.'

'Something perhaps of no great monetary value,' said Frank, 'but rich in human meaning.'

'There's no such thing.'

Ah, but there was. My medal.

'Are you giving her anything, Dad?'

'Yes, I am.'

'What?'

'It's a secret.'

'I hope it isn't anything that belonged to Mom.'

'It isn't.' Though Kate had been proud of my medal.

'Before you go, those Christmas cards on the sideboard came for you.'

There were three. One was from Jean, another from Susan, and the third from Helen Sneddon. Under the seasonable greeting in Helen's was scribbled 'Millie's dead'. That was all, no explanation.

'What's the matter?' asked Madge.

'Nothing. It's all right.'

But, as I went out of the house and got into my car, it was not all right. Had Millie done herself in? If I had stayed at home, could I have saved her? Probably. So, in a way, I was responsible.

7

There was a full muster in the mess for dinner. The Commanding Officer had sent round an order that no one dared disregard, not even the allergic Senator. We all came, dressed for the occasion. The Senator and I wore black dinner jackets, Bolton his blue one with the glittering lapels, and Bliss was in red with gold buttons. As for the ladies, Linda herself was splendidly vulgar in red-and-white velvet, with two strings of pearls round her neck. Her hands sparkled with rings, her ears with earrings, and her hair with a diamond-studded comb. Mrs Bolton wore her plain black dress; her only adornment was her wedding ring. She looked rather more lady-like than her hostess but then, Linda wasn't to be judged by conventional standards. Mrs Hazelwood probably couldn't have told the colour of her dress for, after a day's drinking, she had lapsed into a melancholy stupor. Amantha wore a loose pink skirt down to her ankles and a white blouse, with a big child's bow at the neck. Unfortunately the blouse was see-through and she was wearing no bra. Linda gave her a long grim stare but let her pass.

We were all on our best behaviour, determined not to displease our hostess. No one demurred when we were given our places, though Bliss was placed between the Hazelwoods. On the other side of the table Amantha sat between the Boltons. Linda was at the head of the table, I at the foot; it was if she was hostess and I was host. Bolton winked at me and stuck up his thumb. Bliss gave me a ghastly congratulatory grin. Mrs Bolton smiled approvingly. Mrs Hazelwood looked as if she didn't even know I was there. She had withdrawn into her mind, among God knew what horrifying memories. Her husband kept giving her anxious glances.

I was sorry that Morland was not present. I knew she often ate with Linda, but never when there were guests. That was her own rule, not Linda's. But, thanks to Morland, no doubt, the food was excellent, the wines vintage, and the service faultless.

Linda was as affable as any colonel, but only as long as no one contradicted her.

She saw me smiling. 'What do you find so amusing, Mr Casaubon?' she asked in her Dorothea voice.

They looked puzzled. She explained. 'It's a game the professor and I play. Mr Casaubon is a character in a book.'

'*Middlemarch* by George Eliot,' said Bolton. 'A ponderous work of genius.'

'Go to the top of the class, Josh,' said Linda.

'I read a book once,' said Amantha. 'I forget what it was about.'

'For those of you who do not know the book,' said Linda, 'Casaubon is a clergyman who married a girl half his age. The professor and I were agreed that the marriage was never consummated, Casaubon not having what it takes. So we carried out an experiment to see if we were right.'

'What kind of experiment?' asked Bolton.

'The professor played Casaubon. I played Dorothea. We enacted their wedding-night.'

'Sounds interesting. How did it work out?'

'Tell him, Professor. How did it work out?'

'Very successfully.'

'Speak for yourself. I promised you all a surprise.'

We waited while she took a sip of wine.

'I want you all to tell a story about a Christmas when you were kids.'

'Good,' cried Amantha. 'I like stories.'

'Any objections?' asked Linda.

She looked at each of us in turn. I got the hardest look of all.

'Childhood was a long time ago,' said Bolton. 'I'm glad to have forgotten it.'

'You'll think of something, Josh. Aren't you a famous author? I'll go first.'

I felt alarmed. Which of her many unsuitable stories would she choose?

'Christmas Eve,' she said. 'Like tonight. We were Catholics and dirt-poor.'

'I read in a movie magazine you weren't a Catholic any longer,' said Amantha. 'It said you didn't believe in anything.'

'No interruptions, please. My mother was very devout. Though she couldn't afford it, she gave me and my sister Margarita two cents to go to the church and light candles.'

'Pardon the interruption, Linda,' said Bliss, 'but I never knew you had a sister.'

'No one knew. She died when she was ten, sixty years ago.'

'How sad for you.'

I knew the story she was going to tell. It was in her memoirs. It was one of the parts I had advised her to leave out.

'It was raining,' she said. 'In northern California it often rains in winter. It was chilly too. We were early. The church was empty. It would be packed later for the Christmas Mass. We crept in, knelt at the altar, put in our cents, and lit a candle each. I couldn't help thinking that Jesus on the Cross needed to pee, from the way his knees were pressed together. I was sorry for him. Remember, I was just six. Margarita was on her knees praying. She was very religious. I thought praying was stupid. I thought it was useless. My mother often prayed and nothing good ever happened.

'I heard noises coming from a dark corner. There were lots of dark corners in the church. But I wasn't afraid. I went over to see what the noises were. It was a stone floor and my sandals didn't make any noise. So I was there looking down at them before they knew I was there. I knew what they were doing for I had seen my mother doing it with men. When he knew I was there the man was going to stop but the woman told him to go on, it was all right, she knew my mother. I went back to Margarita, who was still praying. I didn't tell her what I had seen. When I looked over, they were seated as if they had come to worship. They had their hands clasped. The woman was praying. Maybe she was asking Jesus on the Cross to forgive her. When we were leaving the church, the man signed to me to come over. Margarita whispered that we mustn't talk to strangers, not even in church, but I went over and he gave me a whole dollar. He didn't ask me not to tell anyone, he just smiled. I liked him. When I showed the dollar to Margarita she asked why he had given it to me and I said because it was Christmas.'

She took another sip of wine. If it had been blood they couldn't have watched with more horror. They, not I. I watched with admiration and, for the first time, affection.

None of them laughed, but then no one ever laughs at $20,000,000. Linda's money made her inviolable. She could afford to tell the truth.

I was not so fortunate.

Amantha, the simple soul, could say what the others could not. 'Was your mother a prostitute, Mrs Birkenberger?'

'She was also a good Christian.'

Amantha gave that a moment's reflection and then nodded. She had no difficulty in accepting what cleverer people would find impossible.

'Well, that's my Christmas story,' said Linda. 'What's yours, Raimundo?'

'What happened to your sister?' he asked sadly.

'Tuberculosis.'

'Her praying didn't do her any good then, did it?' asked Amantha.

'It did not,' said Linda, grimly meek. 'Well, Raimundo?'

212

'All my Christmases as a child were happy.'

'Tell us about one of them.'

'I was born and brought up in E1 Paso, in Texas. So, you see, I am an American.'

'But Bliss isn't your real name, is it?' asked Mrs Bolton.

'I said no interruptions,' said Linda, 'and no questions.'

'My father was a doctor. He began practice in Mexico City but, when he married my mother, who was an American, he came north and worked among the chicanos of El Paso. I had three brothers and five sisters. I was the youngest. We were very happy, though we were never well-off. Most of my father's patients were poor. At Christmas we didn't hang up stockings. We put our shoes outside the door, as Spanish kids do. Once I found a dead mouse in mine.'

'What a horrible present!' cried Amantha.

'It had a white ribbon round its neck, but its head was bloody where the trap had hit it. My brother Eduardo was responsible. He was fond of practical jokes. He's dead now. They all are.'

Linda broke her own rule and interrupted. 'But you've got dozens of nieces and nephews. You're not alone in the world. Like me.'

'What did you do with it, the mouse I mean?' asked Amantha.

'I put it in a white box and buried it.'

'Did you say a prayer?'

'Yes, I said a prayer.'

'Your turn, Josh,' said Linda.

Bolton smiled. 'My family was Jewish, so Christmas didn't mean much to me. My father was a freethinker. When he got drunk and felt unhappy, he would go and wail at a brewery wall, pretending he was in Jerusalem. I used to creep after him and watch. My mother, though, was very devout. One Christmas, I upset her by going round with a bunch of kids and singing carols. Before my voice broke, I wasn't a bad singer. Some men invited me into a bar and stood me up on the counter and asked me to sing. I sang "Hark, the Herald Angels Sing". I got two dollars and a glass of beer. I had to drink some. I've never liked the taste of beer since.'

'How old were you?' asked Amantha.

'Nine or ten, I guess.'

'No wonder you didn't like the beer.'

'What about you, Senator?' asked Linda. 'You must have had some wonderful Christmases. I mean, your people were rich.'

Hazelwood spoke with a curious diffidence. 'Yes, my father was wealthy. He owned factories that made clothes. Every Christmas he drove round a poor district with presents for children. They took the form of articles of clothing. Once I accompanied him. I would carry a parcel to a door, ring the bell, and run away. If anyone came to the door, I would shout "Merry Christmas!" and sometimes they shouted it back. But once a fellow came to the door, picked up the parcel and ran after me with it. He reached into the car and struck my father across the face. Luckily the parcel contained gloves. At the same time this fellow, he was a black, yelled obscene abuse. Then he began kicking the car and weeping. I shall always remember that black face convulsed with insane hatred. I had bad dreams about it. I think I could say the experience had a permanent effect on me.'

All of us, except Amantha, realised that he had attempted an explanation and an appeal.

'What happened to the gloves?' she asked.

'I don't know. Left on the ground, I suppose. In the snow. Yes, there was snow on the ground.'

'Why was he so angry?'

'I don't know.'

'Maybe one of his kids had just died.'

'Maybe. I remember it as hate, but it could have been grief.'

'You next, Annabel,' said Linda.

Mrs Bolton was eager enough, at first. 'Many of my childhood Christmases were spent in the Governor's mansion. Father

214

Christmas arrived at the door on a sleigh if there was snow, or in a horse carriage if there wasn't. We had a Christmas tree bigger than that one out there. Once, among the children invited was a French princess. We sang a carol in French in her honour. Do you know, when she grew up she married one of the richest men in France, and today is mistress of a magnificent château?'

At that point Mrs Bolton gave up. It was too much for her, the contrast between what she had been then, the Governor's pampered daughter entertaining a princess, and what she was now, the wife of a notorious author, and a mere guest in the house of a fat loud-mouthed domineering rich old Mexican ex-actress, whose mother had been a whore.

'Is it me next?' cried Amantha, who had little patience with middle-aged histrionics.

She spoke with the voice of a pert five-year-old. 'When I was five I was the fairy of the Christmas tree. I don't mean I was up among the branches. I just danced round it. This was on the stage in our city hall. I was picked out of fifty-three. I was dressed all in white and had a shining star on my forehead. I had a wand that I was supposed to do magic with. I would dance about and then I would point my wand to where there was nothing. Then the lights would go out and there would be music. When the lights went on again there, where I had pointed my wand would be a toy, like a doll for a girl or a machine-gun for a boy. Everybody clapped. They said I was better than Shirley Temple at the same age.'

'Well done, sweetie-pie,' cried Bliss.

She simpered and waved her hand, as if it held a wand again.

As if by magic Mrs Hazelwood woke out of her stupor. But perhaps she had been listening all the time.

'Three days before Christmas my father shot himself,' she said.

Leaning across Bliss, her husband entreated her to say no more. She paid him no heed.

'I heard the shot. It came from the library. We still called it

215

that, though the books had all been sold. Everything worth selling had been sold. The house itself was up for sale. My father was lying on the floor. There were no carpets. His head was bloody. I sat down beside him. I got blood on my dress. My father was a nice person. He was the nicest person I've ever known. He was buried on Christmas Day. My mother didn't come to the funeral. I was eight,' she added.

None of us, not even Amantha, asked why her father had done it or why her mother had not gone to the funeral.

Linda broke the silence. She spoke quietly. 'So, Professor, we come to you. As they say, last but not least.'

What a sensation there would have been if I had told the truth.

'In Scotland in those days,' I said, 'Christmas wasn't much celebrated. New Year, or Ne'erday as we called it, was for us the important time.'

'Weren't children given presents at Christmas?' asked Amantha indignantly.

I remembered a pair of boots, almost new, bought at a jumble sale.

'Weren't there parties for children?' she asked.

There were, one for pauper children. Each child given a paper bag with a penny in it, an orange, three sweets wrapped in coloured paper, and a small picture of the King and Queen.

'The four years of the First World War coincided with my childhood,' I said.

'But it wasn't at Christmas that your father, the lawyer, was killed?' asked Linda.

She had ordered that there should be no interruptions, so why was she interrupting me?

'No, that was in September, when the rowans were red. September 1917.'

'What are rowans?' asked Amantha.

'I remember skating one Christmas,' I said. 'It was the

Christmas after my father's death. On a small loch near my home.'

'Near the big stone mansion?' said Linda.

'Not far off. My mother held my hand. She was an expert on skates. She was dressed in black but her cheeks were red. It was a cold dull day. Snow was expected.'

There had been a young woman with red cheeks, skating, but she wasn't my mother. My mother had been at her work in the nail factory.

I wasn't really lying. I was reconstructing the past as it should have been.

'Where was your father killed?' asked Bolton.

'Mesopotamia. He was in the Argylls.'

That last was the truth. I vaguely remembered a tall man in a dark kilt and a glengarry.

Linda was giving me a smile that seemed to have affection in it, or was it pity? What was certain was that it had cruelty in it too.

8

I was in my room, still undressed, when Chung brought a note from Linda. In red ink she had scribbled 'I'd like to see you.' Sick at heart, because of the lies I had told, I would have liked to reply 'Sorry, Linda. Not tonight.' But in that kingdom I was slave, not emperor.

I took out of the drawer the little box containing Bliss's silly purple pills. Here was a crisis in my life. If I took any, it would mean that I was indeed a grubby old fortune-hunter, with no limits to my self-debasement. If I flushed them down the toilet, it wouldn't mean much but I would have regained a little self-respect.

I looked at myself in the mirror. Yes, as Madge had bitterly said, I looked the part. But not the part of the man whom Kate Liddell had loved and married and who now mourned her.

I went outside for a few minutes, to be calmed by the moonlight and the warm scented air, and also to challenge myself to go to Linda and tell her that I had told her cowardly lies. It was not, alas, a serious challenge. I did not have the courage to do it. But if I did not do it I could have no future with Linda.

Suddenly, there was someone beside me. A new scent was in the air. I turned my head. It was Morland, more mysterious than ever. Did she really exist? Was I imagining her? I would have to touch her to prove that she was real. But Morland could not be touched.

'Do you mind if I join you?' she asked.

'Not at all. It's a beautiful night, isn't it?'

Yes, it is.'

'Don't you go home for Christmas?'

'This is my home.'

'Yes, of course. Where do your parents live?'

'My mother's dead. My father remarried. He lives in Boston.'

'Was that where you were born?'

'Yes.'

It was also where she had killed a man and where she had spent seven years in prison.

'It's a lot colder there,' I said.

'There's snow on the ground now.'

'In Lunderston we don't usually get snow till after the New Year.'

There was a pause.

'It's not too late, Mr McLeod,' she said.

She was again warning me.

'You could slip away without anyone knowing.'

'And go where?'

'To your daughter's.'

'Who would drive me?'

'Yourself. The car could be recovered later.'

Was she jealous, afraid that she would lose her place as Linda's confidante?

'If I choose to stay, what's going to happen?' I asked.

'I'm sorry, I can't tell you that.'

Had she promised Linda?

'Has Mrs Birkenberger got a surprise for me?' I asked.

'You could call it that.'

'But not a pleasant one?'

She did not answer.

Seconds later, she was gone.

What could the unpleasant surprise be? I thought I could guess. After the Christmas meal I was to be kicked out. It would be done ruthlessly and publicly. I was to be shown up as a grubby old fortune-hunter. I was to be laughed at.

I should have taken Morland's advice.

Instead, I made my way to Linda's room.

This time I knocked on the door.

'Come in,' she called.

I went in. She was seated at the dressing-table, rubbing white cream over her face. She was like a Papuan head-hunter.

'You took your time,' she said, affably enough.

'I went outside for a smoke.'

I could not tell whether she was smiling or scowling.

'Sit down,' she said.

I sat down.

'How many minutes to Christmas?'

I looked at my watch. 'Fifteen.'

'They're just arriving at the stable.'

'Yes.'

'The world's about to get its Saviour.'

'That's the story.'

'From now on, goodness and truth are going to prevail.'

'That was the idea.'

'Have you anything to tell me?'

'Do you mean what I've decided about Josh and Raimundo?'

'That too, but something else.'

What was that something else?

'I'm not sure I know what you're talking about, Linda.'

'You should know. I think you do know.'

I tried to make a joke of it. 'In this room, I'm not sure whether I'm to be Casaubon or myself.'

'Yourself? Now that's an interesting subject. Who's yourself?'

I was aware of the absurd American obsession with identity. They were always trying to find out who they were.

'Do you know your real self, Professor?'

'I thought you'd given up calling me Professor.'

'Sorry. What's your name again?'

'Gregor.'

'Do you know your real self, Gregor? All my life I've been in search of mine.'

'Did you never find it?'

'It's not a joke.' She said it mildly.

'No. But does it matter?'

'It matters a lot. It's very ignorant of you to say it doesn't matter.'

'If you found it, Linda, how would you know it was your real identity?'

'My true identity is me as God sees me, with all the lies scraped off.'

'I thought you didn't believe in God.'

'I've never said that. When did I ever say I didn't believe in God?'

'If I want to know the truth about myself, Linda, I don't need God to tell me. All I have to do is to go and stand in front of Rembrandt.'

'You mean the painting?'

'Yes, the self-portrait. In it, he has so honestly told the truth about himself that anyone looking at it feels obliged to tell the truth too.'

'Tell me then.'

'Tell you what?'

'The truth about yourself.'

I had almost fallen into a trap. 'I can't do that, Linda. I can tell the truth about myself only to myself, not to anyone else. I'd need Rembrandt's genius to do that. It's not a matter of words. It's got to do with secret thoughts and feelings. Words are limited in what they can say.'

'They can say plenty if you want them to say it.'

'Take Mrs Hazelwood, for instance. There she was at dinner telling us about her father. We saw her, we heard her, but we were an infinite distance from knowing what was going on in her mind. There are things that are incommunicable, at any rate in our present state of mental development.'

'You're talking as if we were apes. This is a very convenient theory, if there are things you want to hide. Is it midnight yet?'

'A minute past.'

'So it's Christmas Day?'

'Yes. Merry Christmas, Linda.'

'You can tell me now whether I've to give the money to Josh or Raimundo.'

'This is a very invidious task you've given me.'

'I'm not sure what "invidious" means, but I asked you to do it and you agreed to do it.'

'I'd like to back out, if you don't mind.'

'I do mind. You can't back out.'

'Give the money to them both then. You can easily afford it.'

'You're very generous with my money.'

'Then give it to neither of them.'

'Now you're being mean. Which one? Josh or Raimundo? There's nothing incommunicable about that.'

'It's unfair to both of them. I don't really know them.'

'They know about it. They've accepted it.'

No doubt, it would please her if I were to nominate Bliss, but I just could not. Though he was a kinder person than I and more forgiving, I still saw him as a diseased old lecher, a debaucher of young girls. I wanted the loan sharks to get him.

'Josh,' I said.

She didn't hesitate for a second. 'Josh it is, then. Let Annabel have her pearls. Let Raimundo be thrown to the sharks.'

'That's not fair, Linda.'

'I'll give Josh the good news myself. You'll give Raimundo the bad news.'

'I'd rather not.'

'In the gallery, tomorrow at ten, in front of Rembrandt. I'll send word to him to meet you there. Good night.'

I wished her good night and crept away.

I crept, but all was not yet lost. I wasn't looking forward to the meeting with Bliss but I wasn't dreading it either. I was sure Rembrandt would have shared my opinion of the old roué. And would Linda have put me through that catechism if she didn't have some regard for me, some respect, some liking even? As for Morland's warning, why should I heed a woman not quite right in the head? I remembered her naked appeal to the moon.

9

At breakfast, there was an exchange of seasonable greetings, not all of them sincere.

Josh Bolton was as jolly as Father Christmas. He even went out of his way to greet Senator Hazelwood with gleeful cordiality. He had been told by Linda that, thanks to me, he was to get his loan. That was one reason for his jolliness, the other was that he had learned from a telephone call to a friend in Washington just how desperate the Senator's financial plight was.

We talked on the terrace, beside the Christmas tree. Its baubles tinkled.

'Do you know why he needs that money?' he asked.

'Isn't it for investment in a company that he's got an interest in?'

'That's just a blind. He needs at least two million to keep him out of prison. They've caught up with the bastard at last. He's misappropriated money belonging to other people and he can't make it good. He's tried everywhere. Even the President's turned his back on him.'

'If he really is in danger of going to prison, won't Linda take pity on him?'

Hazelwood that morning had looked sickly but had tried to be polite and dignified. He had even shaken hands with Bliss.

Mrs Hazelwood had kept to her room.

'Not a chance,' said Bolton. 'Look how he's treated Bliss like shit. Mind you, that's how Bliss should be treated, but not when Linda's looking. Annabel and I think it was bloody gutsy of you to give the money to me.'

'I didn't give it to you, Josh. It wasn't mine to give. Besides, isn't it a loan, to be paid back eventually?'

'Sure.'

'Bliss could never have paid it back. You can, though. All you have to do is write another best-seller like *Blood on the Ground*.'

'Sure, that's all. Nothing to it. I've already got it written in my head. Have you told the old cunt yet?'

'No.' I looked at my watch. 'In ten minutes I've to meet him in the picture gallery.'

'Was that Linda's arrangement?'

'Yes.'

'Isn't she the sadistic old bitch. Look out, Gregor. She knows how Bliss covets those paintings.'

'I've been told he admires them.'

'Same thing.'

Bliss was waiting for me in the gallery. Morland had let him in.

He greeted me eagerly. His cheeks had been freshly rouged. He was wearing a cravat, the colour of blood. It looked as if his throat had been cut.

Enthusiastically he pointed out felicities of colour and design. When he came to the Rembrandt self-portrait, he greeted it as an old friend.

'Have you seen it before?' I asked, jealously.

'Heavens, yes, dozens of times. Old Van Djinn and I know each other well. Look, he's winking at me.'

He wasn't, of course, but he did look sardonically amused.

'His wife Saskia died when she was only twenty-nine. He loved her. He painted her many times. She was like my Amantha, only fatter. In those days, a woman had to be fat to be thought beautiful. He was often in financial difficulties, like me. They say no painter has ever depicted human beings with more sympathy, especially if they were old. If he had painted me, as I am now, he would have made me look like a dying old clown, which is what I am, but he wouldn't have done it spitefully. People looking at it might not have respected me but they would have liked me, which is much better. Don't you think so, Gregor?'

I had to nod. I myself liked him but did not respect him.

'It's worth at least fifty million dollars, a thousand times more than he earned all his life. Look, he sees the joke.'

'In your own lifetime, Raimundo, you must have earned a great deal.'

He grinned like a small boy accused of a misdeed that he was rather proud of.

'Millions?' I said.

'Oh yes, millions.'

'What happened to it? I believe you never married.'

'True, but I had many sweethearts, frequently more than one at a time; an expensive hobby. It was my good fortune to be attractive to many women.'

'Why did you never get married?'

'And restrict myself to one? Being a good Catholic, I would have had to be faithful. Besides, I have always abhorred domesticity. I like children but I would have hated to be a father. Isn't that silly?'

I spoke sternly. 'People seeing you with Amantha would take her to be your granddaughter.'

'The older I get, the younger I need my women to be. Rembrandt understands, as you can see.'

Gregor McLeod understood too but strongly disapproved. If there had to be lechery in old age, at least let it be decent. A girl of 19 in the skinny embrace of a man of 75 was an abomination. If it wasn't mentioned in Leviticus, it ought to have been. That he was probably impotent somehow made it more abominable, not less. But was he impotent? Could this moribund and desiccated creature still manage it, with the help of his little purple pills? If he could, it would be good news for septuagenarians, but nonetheless loathsome to imagine.

He turned from Rembrandt to me. 'Well, Gregor, is this the moment of truth? Linda said you would tell me here what you had decided.'

'First of all, Raimundo, I would like to say that I pleaded with Linda to relieve me of this responsibility. I told her I had no right to make the choice. It was none of my business.'

'But, surely, if you are to be her sixth, it is your business.'

'Am I to be her sixth?'

'It's what she has been leading us all to believe.'

Suddenly I felt joyful and triumphant, as in the carol.

Boldly I faced him. 'You can see the impossible position I was in, Raimundo. I did not know you or Josh. I had seen some of your films and read one or two of his books but I knew nothing of you both personally. So what I did was cut cards. This is for Raimundo I said and cut. It was the nine of diamonds. (Did I choose that card because in Scotland it is a symbol for treachery?) This is for Josh, I said, and cut. It was the jack of hearts. Blame chance, not me. I'm sorry, Raimundo.'

He shut his eyes, turned pale, opened them again, smiled, and held out his hand. I had to take it. It felt like a dead man's.

'Fair enough,' he said. 'I'm happy for Josh.'

'I suggested to her that both of you should be given the loans you needed. I pointed out she could easily afford it. I'm afraid she refused.'

'She has always had a playful streak in her.'

'Some would call it a sadistic streak.'

Immediately, I regretted saying that. At the moment Bliss seemed to think he was in a film acting the part of a man courageous and forgiving in the face of unjust adversity, but in an hour or so, back in the real world, he might sneak off to Linda and tell her I had called her sadistic. It was what a piqued child would have done and that was what he was, for all his 75 years and his many lovers.

10

Christmas dinner was to be at three o'clock on the terrace, beside the tree. Dress was to be informal. Paper hats were to be worn. Guests would sit where they pleased. These were the orders issued by Linda and conveyed by her aide de camp Morland.

In the morning I relaxed by the pool with the Boltons. They kept thanking me for choosing them and congratulating me for disappointing Bliss.

The Hazelwoods were in their room, skulking according to Josh. He said we'd to keep listening for a shot. It would be the Senator following his father-in-law's example.

I said I hoped not, for Mrs Hazelwood's sake. Surely she had had enough of spilt brains.

Amantha was lying on a lilo in the pool. She had told us that Bliss was in his room writing letters. I thought he was more likely than the Senator to shoot himself. But he would aim at his heart. He wouldn't trust any mortician to build up his face again.

'By the way, Gregor,' said Annabel, 'Linda told us she was off to Acapulco next week. She didn't say she was going alone but that was the impression we got. Wasn't it, darling?'

'Sure was. The lady's not short of virile companions down there.'

'What will you do, Gregor?' asked Annabel. 'Will you go back home to Scotland?'

She smiled sweetly but her eyes were sour with spite. Gratitude could show itself in strange ways.

I saw myself through her eyes, through the eyes of the

Governor's daughter. She saw me as a lackey, a sponger, a pathetic hanger-on.

She was right. That was what I was in this place.

I shut my eyes and had a memory of home.

A day or two before Christmas. A winter game of golf. A day dry, but cold. Dusk falling quick and chilly. The Cumbrae lighthouse flashing out on the dark Firth. A drink afterwards in the clubhouse. One only, for I was eager to get home to Kate. The lamplit streets and avenues of Lunderston. Putting the car in the garage, a neat manoeuvre, for the garage was small and the car large. Going into the house by the back door. Kate in the bright warm kitchen preparing the tea. Homely smell of cooking. Kate herself lovely and warm in lambswool, with an apron on which were depicted in colour scenes of Scotland: Loch Lomond, Ben Nevis, Inveraray Castle. Kissing her, casually it seemed, but letting her know she meant more to me than anyone else on earth. Taking a shower. Changing. In the living-room, pouring out a sherry for her, a malt for me. Going into the kitchen with them. Chatting. About anything at all. Feeling wonderfully happy and safe.

I opened my eyes and wondered where I was. There was a woman bending down and speaking to me. Her accent was alien. She wasn't Kate. Kate was dead.

It was Mrs Hazelwood. She was asking if she could have a word in private.

'Yes, of course,' I said, still bemused. I stood up.

The Boltons were looking on in astonishment.

Amantha was giving me a wave.

'Shall we go to the library?' I said.

Among the books we sat down. Her hands were shaky. She tried to smile pleasantly.

I had guessed what it was she wanted to talk about. She was under the delusion that I had influence with Linda. Perhaps too she had seen on my face pity mixed with horror when she had been talking about her father shooting himself. She thought I was compassionate. But, as I had shown in another library, my compassion was a feeble thing.

'Leonard and I heard just this morning, Mr McLeod, that you lost your wife recently. The housekeeper Morland told us. We were both very sorry to hear it.'

'Thank you.'

'No doubt you have been told why Leonard and I have come here.'

I nodded. 'Yes, I've been told.'

'But perhaps not accurately or sympathetically.'

I thought of the clinic in Baton Rouge.

'My husband is a good man. You will have been told lies about him. He has many enemies. They wish to see him disgraced.'

As a foreigner I felt I had no right to comment.

'Mrs Birkenberger was once married to a very good friend of my husband's. She herself became our friend, or so we thought. That is why we have come here to ask her for help. The sum of money involved is quite a large one, but she could easily afford it. Leonard would be able to pay it back in less than a year, with interest. If he does not get it he may go to prison. She has refused.'

Her voice had become hoarse, her eyes were bloodshot. She desperately needed a drink.

'We have reason to believe you have influence with her, Mr McLeod.'

'Who told you that?'

'She did herself. She gave us to believe that you and she might be getting married.'

'That's not true,' I muttered.

'You're our last hope, Mr McLeod.'

But, lady, I wanted to say, this for me is dreamland. This house, its mistress, the sums of money mentioned, millions of dollars, they don't really exist. Reality for me is a small kitchen in a small house far away, with my wife Kate.

But Kate was dead.

'Will you at least speak to her, Mr McLeod?'

I remembered the lynched Negro, the man with his brains blown out on the carpetless floor, and the disowned grandchildren. I should have spurned her but I heard myself saying, 'All right, I'll speak to her, but I don't think it will do any good.'

'Thank you, Mr McLeod.'

She went off then, trying not to hurry, but desperate for a drink.

I went straight to Linda's private quarters. If I had hesitated, I wouldn't have gone.

'Who is it?' she called, impatiently I thought, when I knocked.

'It's me, Gregor.'

'Oh. Come in.' She didn't sound very welcoming.

I went in.

She had her spectacles on and was studying documents spread out on a table. I had always suspected she was a capable business woman.

She pushed the spectacles up onto her forehead. 'Well, what is it?'

She was wearing a white blouse and red pants.

'Sorry if I'm intruding,' I mumbled.

'You are intruding. Have you something to tell me?'

'Yes, I have. After Christmas dinner I shall be returning to my daughter and her family.'

I hadn't known myself seconds ago that I was going to say that.

'I see,' she said.

'I've done all I can for your memoirs. Perhaps you should get an expert to look at them.'

'That's already been arranged. Is there anything else?'

'Yes. Mrs Hazelwood has just been speaking to me.'

'Was she sober enough to make sense?'

'She told me that her husband would probably be disgraced and imprisoned if he couldn't raise a certain sum of money.'

'Did she say how much that certain sum of money was?'

'I believe two million.'

'You believe right. Have you got two million?'

'Of course not.'

'Then it's none of your business.'

'I told her so.'

'Why, then, have you come here, bothering me? You had no right.'

'I know that.'

'If you did have two million, would you give it to him?'

'If I had twenty million, I might. For the sake of his daughter.'

'You don't know his daughter.'

'I just think she might not want her father to go to prison.'

'I don't think she'd mind.'

'Have you met her?'

'Yes, I have. She despises him.'

And you, Linda, despise me. 'Sorry for bothering you,' I muttered and left.

In my abjectness, I felt that I ought to have waited for permission to leave.

I wanted to go straight to my room but Mrs Hazelwood waylaid me. She had a glass in her hand. She had given in. Her hope had not been strong enough.

'I'm sorry,' I said. 'She wasn't interested.'

11

What I should have done was telephone Madge, tell her Christmas dinner at Linda's was cancelled, and that I would be home directly.

I didn't, because I couldn't bring myself to quit dreamland and return to reality. That, though, wasn't the reason I gave myself. It would be a pity, I told myself, to disappoint Frank Junior and Midge and also there was still a chance that Frank could get the account. It was the sort of contemptuous gesture that would appeal to Linda. I had just seen how she liked demonstrating the power over people that her wealth gave her.

I stayed in my room till two o'clock, which was the time Madge and her family were due to arrive.

The Boltons were on the terrace, with gleeful news. The Hazelwoods had gone. Miguel had taken them to the airport. Linda hadn't bothered to say goodbye. It just needed Bliss to drop down dead for the Christmas dinner to be a really joyful occasion.

To my alarm, when Frank's car appeared, so did Linda, coming out of the house to greet them. She was dressed simply in a long loose yellow dress, with a minimum of jewellery. I was afraid she might insult them in some way, but no, good actress that she was, she put on a display of hospitality that, I noticed, disconcerted Madge. My proud daughter had come prepared to make it clear she had come out of courtesy and was not going to enjoy herself, but she couldn't help being won over by Linda's friendliness, especially towards Frank Junior and Midge. They were enchanted by the famous, beautiful, and charming Linda Blossom, and impressed by the magnificence of her house and grounds.

Linda was nice to me too. She called me Gregor and complimented me on having such mannerly and handsome grandchildren.

Frank Junior, introduced to Bolton, was dutifully over-whelmed. He showed an acquaintance with Bolton's books that greatly pleased the author.

Midge asked me, in a whisper, where Raimundo Bliss was; she was eager to meet that legendary lover. He was, I supposed, having his warpaint put on by his attendant squaw, but I didn't say it. I said that he would appear shortly. He wasn't very well and needed rest.

My son-in-law, wearing a blue bow tie, expressed disappoint-ment that he was not going to meet Senator Hazelwood. 'It's not every day one gets a chance to meet one of the great men of our country.' Linda laughed and said not everyone had that opinion of the Senator.

Very soon Frank Junior and Midge, who had brought their swimming costumes, were in the big pool. As they swam about, they gave me waves. I had gone up in their estimation.

Madge remembered she had brought Linda a present. 'Will you go and get it, Frank?'

Frank ran down the steps to the car and came back with a thin packet wrapped in brown paper.

It turned out to be a calender with scenes of Scotland in colour. One was of Prince Charlie's Bay on the small Hebridean island of Eriskay. 'Do you remember it, Dad?' asked Madge.

Did she really think I might have forgotten? We had spent a holiday there, 40 or so years ago. Kate had been in her 30s then, sunburnt, with her hair yellower than ever with the sun. How happy she had been, playing with her two girls on the sand. The islanders, every one of them Catholic, had invited her to attend their church service. She had gone, with five-year-old Jean. Madge and I, stubborn Presbyterians, had preferred to climb a hill.

'Yes, Kate,' I said, 'I remember it well.'

If anyone noticed it, no one corrected my mistake, if it was a mistake.

Just then Bliss and Amantha appeared, hand in hand.

They were wearing Christmas hats, his pink in the shape of a crown, hers a red coronet. Not able to show on his ravaged face the jolliness of Christmas, he had thought the silly hat would do it. He looked ghastly. I was sure he was in pain.

Amantha knew that he was ill, she must have seen him taking painkillers and she must have heard his gasps, but she was only 19, it was Christmas, and she had a right to enjoy herself, so she rushed off to join Frank Junior and Midge in the pool.

'I believe the Senator and his wife have gone,' said Bliss. 'What a pity!'

He really meant it.

'How are you feeling, Raimundo?' asked Linda anxiously.

'Fine. I'm feeling fine. I did take a nasty little turn half an hour ago, but I've quite recovered, thank you.'

The next nasty little turn, which might happen at any moment, would probably do for him.

Being introduced to Madge and Frank, he said how pleased he was to meet Gregor's relatives. He meant that too.

Madge had frowned when she had seen how young and guileless Amantha was, and she still greatly disapproved, but she couldn't help responding to his childlike eagerness to be excused and liked.

If he drops dead, I thought, with his last breath he'll ask that the festivities be not disturbed.

Once, so discreetly that only I, his executioner, noticed, he crossed himself, perhaps remembering Christmas in El Paso many years ago.

But the happiest person there was my son-in-law, the banker. He was having Christmas dinner with a millionairess, in her $3,000,000 lair. This was heaven on earth.

The meal was a buffet. Long tables were laden with a variety of food and drink. Chung and the two little maids were there to help. So was Morland, but she was also a guest, entitled to wear a silly hat. With our heaped plates and filled glasses, we sat at one or other of the small tables. Amantha sat with Frank Junior but alas, he was more interested in the turkey's breast than in hers. He liked food and here was a feast. He also liked wine and there was an abundance, of a quality he would never be able to afford. When his mother shook her head reprovingly after his third glass, he grinned and raised it, toasting her. She had to smile. He was her son, he was enjoying himself, and it was Christmas. I thought that, as a student of philosophy, Frank Junior might not score high marks in written examinations but, in practice, he had an attitude that Socrates would have approved: know yourself, and then look after yourself.

I wished I had given Frank Junior my medal. But there it was on the tree, with Linda's name on the tag. I wondered if I could, when no one was looking, snatch it down and stick it in my pocket. Giving it to Linda was an act of gross sycophancy. I deserved to be laughed at. I remembered Helen Sneddon accusing me of showing off.

Midge was asking Bliss lots of questions about his career as a film star. She was wearing the scant costume she had swum in.

Madge and Frank sat with the Boltons. I sat with Morland.

Wearing a long white dress, she was the only one there whom the paper hat did not make look ridiculous. But nothing could ever have done that. I couldn't resist asking her if it was true that Linda was going to Acapulco shortly. She smiled and nodded. I did resist asking if I would be invited.

Everybody heard Amantha tell Frank Junior that Mrs Birkenberger always gave valuable presents to her guests at Christmas. Raimundo had told her.

Except for Morland, none of us, not even Madge, was absolutely sober when Linda stood up in our midst and announced that it was time for the giving of presents.

Only Amantha clapped, which meant that only Amantha was honest. The rest of us tried to look as if a present from a millionairess did not interest us. We were being well bred.

I found myself, bloody fool that I was, on my feet. I have a present for you, Linda,' I said.

I went to the tree and took down the small box. I brought it back and handed it to Linda. 'With my best wishes,' I said stupidly.

Madge was looking suspicious and cross. Probably she thought that in the small box was a piece of jewellery that had belonged to her mother.

Linda removed the gift paper, opened the box, and took out the medal with its ribbon attached. 'What the hell's this?' she cried, holding it up by the ribbon like a dead fish.

'It's your Military Medal, Dad,' cried Madge.

'For kissing the colonel's ass,' cried Bolton.

'It says,' said Linda, 'for gallantry.'

'I didn't know you were a hero, Grandad,' cried Midge, laughing.

'It should be Frank Junior's,' said Madge.

'So it should,' said Linda and, going over to him, handed him the medal.

I couldn't have felt more ashamed if I had been caught cheating at golf.

'Midge,' said Linda, 'there's a red envelope on the tree with your name and your brother's on it.'

Midge was at the tree almost before Linda had finished speaking. Her sharp acquisitive eyes quickly spotted the envelope. She snatched it down and ran over to Frank Junior with it. She ripped it open, with Amantha stretching forward to look. It was she who, in awe, shouted out the amount written on the cheques. 'A thousand dollars!'

Frank Junior, with my medal pinned on his chest, had a big happy grin.

Midge rushed over to Linda and gave her a hug.

Their mother wasn't pleased. In Lunderston too-expensive presents were deprecated as bad taste.

I looked at Linda and she looked at me. 'You are trying to buy our souls,' my look said, and hers replied, 'Yes, and am I not succeeding?'

Amantha was next. Her present was a book. She couldn't hide her disgust. Did Mrs Birkenberger not know she never read books? What could you do with a book? I was sure it was *Middlemarch* and was really a message for me. But what message?

Bliss tried to console his sweetie-pie. 'There are two kinds of riches,' he croaked, bravely. 'The material and the spiritual. The latter are infinitely superior. You have been paid a great compliment, my pet.'

But Amantha had discovered what you did with a book. You held it upside down and shook it. Out fluttered a cheque. She seized it, looked at it, and gave a squeal of joy. Then she rushed over to Linda and kissed her on the cheek. If ever there was a soul ready to be bought, it was Amantha's.

'Raimundo, you're next,' said Linda.

Because he was too weak and ill, and also too tipsy, she went to the tree on his behalf and brought back a small envelope. She opened it for him and took out, not a cheque, but a small sheet of paper with something typed on it.

He took it in his palsied hands, thanked her, and read it. Ghastly before, his face turned whiter still, and more corpselike. His voice, when he managed to speak, was hoarse. 'Really, Linda, I cannot accept.'

'Yes, you can and you will. I was going to give them all to the Museum anyway. Why shouldn't you have one?'

She then rather truculently satisfied our curiosity. 'Raimundo is to have his pick of my paintings, except the Rembrandt.'

Bolton expressed all our astonishment. 'Jesus Christ!' he cried.

He and I had discussed the paintings. Not one was worth less than a million dollars. Not only would Bliss be able to appease the loan sharks, he would also be able to afford another Amantha or two, if he lived that long.

He wasn't altogether overjoyed. 'This is the most munificent present, Linda, but what am I to do with it?'

'Anything you like.'

'Of course, I would love to keep it. It would be an inspiration.'

'Then keep it.'

But she knew he couldn't afford to keep it.

Was the gift, therefore, as much an act of cruelty as of kindness? Not in this case surely. She was genuinely fond of Bliss.

'I'd like the Matisse, with the blue flowers,' he said. 'It's so pure.'

'Sell it to the Museum. Then you can still see it.'

'Yes, I could do that.'

The painted old bugger was weeping. Dark tears streamed down his rouged cheeks.

Linda returned to the giving of presents.

The Boltons had already had theirs: that 'loan' of $100,000.

Madge and Frank, it seemed, were to get none. Perhaps, though, Frank would get the account. He would be told less publicly.

I hoped that I too would get nothing. I did not trust Linda. I remembered Morland's warnings.

'Your turn, Gregor,' said Linda.

So it was Gregor. Not Mr Casaubon. Not Professor. Perhaps I was being unfair to her. Perhaps she did wish me well and was about to show it.

'Your present is the truth,' she said.

Everybody looked puzzled, except Amantha who was interested only in her cheque and what it could buy.

241

What the hell was Linda up to? How could anyone be presented with the truth? The truth about what?

I went to the tree briskly. There was a buff envelope with my name on it, the sort of envelope that might contain a document. The letters MM and MA were after my name. Not even the Inland Revenue did that.

It could, conceivably, contain a marriage proposal drawn up by lawyers, with my portion strictly limited.

I took out a letter, on paper as stiff as a document, three pages of it.

The sky was blue, beautiful, and neutral. There was no help anywhere. I was on my own.

Madge tried to come to my rescue. 'Whatever it is, Dad, you don't have to read it here.'

'Yes, Grandad,' cried Midge, read it to us.'

Her trust had been bought.

To my astonishment, the address at the top was Hope Street, Glasgow. It was from a firm of private investigators, Cameron & McLean. The subject was Mr Gregor McLeod, MM MA of 144 Goatfell Avenue, Lunderston, Ayrshire.

So Linda, behind my back, had used the magic of money to expose my lies.

It was no big deal. Weren't Americans proud that their greatest President had been born in a log cabin? No doubt, as a boy, Abraham Lincoln had shat in an outside lavatory.

But there was one secret that I hoped Cameron & McLean, no matter how big their fee, had not been able to dig up.

Excusing myself, I hurried off, as if to empty my bladder. Indeed, the first thing I did when I got to my room was relieve myself.

Then, by the window, with bougainvillea on the sill, I read the truth about my childhood.

'The subject, Mr Gregor McLeod, was born in Dechmont, a village in the county of Lanark, about ten miles from Glasgow, on 11th September, 1912. It was then a rural district, though with several coal mines, all but one of which were defunct during Mr McLeod's childhood.'

I remembered sliding down the huge bings on a sledge of corrugated iron.

'The houses were mostly small tenements. Today they have all gone. High-rise blocks of flats have taken their place. Not a brick remains of the building where Mr McLeod was born.'

Once, while Kate was shopping in Glasgow, I had sneaked out to visit Dechmont for the first time in many years. Every trace of my childhood had been removed, not only the building where I had been born but also the shops against whose windows I had pressed my nose, looking in at all the things I could not afford to buy.

'We were fortunate to find two old women who had lived in the district all their lives and remembered Mr McLeod and his family well. From them we obtained most of the following information. Their accounts tallied in most respects.'

Was one of them Bella McDaid who had been my sweetheart when I was six? We had walked to school hand in hand. She had worn red stockings. Her father had been a railway porter.

'The tenement in which Mr McLeod was born and where he lived till he was 12 stood on the bank of a stream which gave it its name, Burnbank Terrace. The houses were either of two apartments, called room-and-kitchens, or one apartment, called single-ends. All the toilets were outside, shared by two, or in some cases three, families.'

Yes, but, if your need was desperate, you could use other people's.

Nothing was said about the profusion of white butterflies and the bumble bees, the sodgers as we called them with the khaki stripes and the fuggies that had no sting.

What was being reported was the dull prose of my childhood,

with all the poetry left out. Whatever she had paid, Linda had not got the truth.

'Most of the inhabitants of Dechmont worked in the remaining mine or the steelworks or a factory that made nails. A few were farm labourers. Mr McLeod's father was a labourer in the steelworks, and his wife, before her marriage, worked in the nail factory. Mr McLeod Senior never enjoyed good health but that did not prevent him from being called up in 1917.

'After demobilisation in 1919, Mr McLeod returned to the steelworks but, in less than a year, he died of rheumatic fever. No pension was granted his wife, though it was widely believed that his wartime hardships had fatally impaired his health. Unable to find work, Mrs McLeod was obliged to seek parish relief, in American terms welfare, to support her two sons, Gregor, then eight, and Stanley, five. It must have been a bitter pill for her to swallow because, according to our informants, she was a quiet proud hard-working woman.'

Was Linda, I wondered, reminded of her own mother? She too had suffered without complaint. Had it not lent her dignity?

I did not feel angry with Linda. On the contrary, I felt grateful. Thanks to her, I was being made to remember my mother honestly. I saw her clearly in my mind: small, a rather big nose reddened by dyspepsia, slightly deaf from the racket in the nail factory, hands rough with work and chapped with chilblains.

Dignity? Could that big word be applied to her? She was, I now realised, the most dignified person I had ever known.

Tears were in my eyes. It was all past. I could never make amends.

'The boys were issued with parish clothing.'

With silk against my neck now, I remembered the grey jersey with the red stripes on the collar that were the giveaway. It had irritated my skin and lacerated my soul.

244

'By this time, Gregor was being spoken of by his teachers as a very clever boy.'

The old schoolmaster in the carpet slippers – what was his name? Mr Richards – had summoned my mother to tell her what a pity it was that so promising a pupil would not get the chance of success that his abilities deserved. 'He'll get it,' she had replied, and she had kept her word.

Too readily I had accepted her self-sacrifice, and I had never shown gratitude. It wasn't so much that I wasn't good at showing it – though I wasn't – it was more that she wasn't good at receiving it. She was too proud.

'Subsequently, Mrs McLeod got her old job back in the nailworks. She had a reputation as a skilful reliable worker. There she worked till 1929, when the factory closed. By that time, Gregor, having won bursaries, was a pupil at Cadzow Academy, the most prestigious school in the county, where most of the pupils paid fees.'

Though my mother was then earning a reasonable wage and giving me more than my share – no wonder Stanley had been jealous – I was probably the poorest boy in the school, but to my credit I never cringed or looked sorry for myself. Indeed, I had begun to acquire a way of carrying myself more suited to a duchess's son than a factory worker's. My skin, though, was never as thick as I pretended. It helped that I was good at sports, especially cricket.

'Mrs McLeod soon found a post as cook-housekeeper to a retired civil servant in Glasgow. The two boys went to live with a maiden aunt in the nearby town of Lightburn. Her house was in a dilapidated tenement.'

Aunt Annie was my father's sister. Her great wish was to be buried in Skye, home of her ancestors. She had some Gaelic and liked to sing Gaelic songs. She was a feckless soul but she did her best for us. She wasn't buried in Skye. It would have cost too much. Perhaps by that time I could have afforded it, but what would have been the use? In any case, I didn't learn that she was dead till long afterwards.

'Gregor had to face some persecution. He was often jeered at and called names.'

Yes, but many of those who had jeered had really been paying me tribute. Stuck in the mire of poverty and ignorance themselves, they could not help respecting someone struggling to get out of it.

'Gregor did well at university.'

I could have got a good honours degree in English if I had been able to afford the extra year. My mother's employer, the retired civil servant, had died, and the people who now employed her, a doctor and his wife, did not pay her so well.

'At teachers' training college, Gregor did particularly well. He was the most outstanding student of his year.'

The test lessons by which the prospective teachers were judged had really been exhibitions of showing off. None had been better at that than I.

'As a consequence, at a time when many students could not find teaching posts, Gregor was appointed to Afton Primary School in Gantock. There he met Katherine Liddell, daughter of a Gantock doctor, and within a year they were married. It would appear that his mother was greatly disappointed at his marrying so soon. She had hoped that he would provide a home for her and Stanley. We have no evidence that she was present at the wedding, which took place in the Mid Kirk in Gantock on 30th June, 1937.'

She had not been invited because I had convinced myself that she would not be comfortable among Kate's superior relations and friends. I also assured myself that she would have refused. She was thrawn, as well as proud. Kate had thought it strange that my mother wasn't there, but she had not insisted.

'About that time, Stanley, a joiner, aged 22, emigrated to New Zealand. He wanted his mother to accompany him but she was not willing. Probably she was too ill to make such a long journey.'

Stanley never forgave me. I wrote to him once but he didn't reply. I heard later, from some source or other, that he had married a Maori woman.

'Gregor's first child, a daughter called Margaret after his wife's mother, was born in 1941, not long before he was called up. He served in North Africa in the Royal Corps of Signals. He won a Military Medal for bravery in the field.

'It was about this time that his mother died, in unknown circumstances. He was not able to come home for the funeral.'

Would anyone believe that I had never once sought out that grave? Shame kept me away, but again Kate had not insisted. My mother was never mentioned in our house. Kate had kept silent because she had seen that I wanted her to keep silent. There was no photograph of my mother on display.

Kate had never met my mother.

There was a knock on the door.

'Come in,' I called.

I thought it was Madge, come to find out what was the matter.

It was Linda.

'I've not come to apologise,' she said.

'Why should you apologise? As you Americans say, I had it coming to me.'

'So you had.'

'I suppose you think I should go and read it out to them. They'll be wondering.'

'I told them it was a contract giving you twelve per cent of royalties from my book. I think they believed me.'

'But, Linda, that was a lie.'

She smiled. 'So it was.'

'They left out the best bits or, should I say, the worst bits.'

'Who did?'

247

'Cameron and McLean. They left out how I betrayed my mother.'

'I wouldn't say they left it out.'

'They treated it too superficially.'

'Well, you can put that right now. I'm willing to listen.'

So I told her. I portrayed myself as a liar, a braggart, a poseur, a moral coward, and a callous ingrate.

She didn't interrupt me once.

'I know how you feel,' she said when I was finished.

I saw in her eyes that she really did know.

Perhaps it wasn't too late for either of us. We could help each other to find redemption.

But she was going to Acapulco and I was returning to Scotland.

CHILDISH THINGS

The author of *The Cone-Gatherers* (1955) and *Fergus Lamont* (1979), both classics of twentieth-century Scottish literature, continues to delight his reading public with excellent new fiction. Robin Jenkins was born in Cambuslang in 1912. His first novel was published in 1951 and more than twenty-five works of fiction have followed, many of which have been graced with literary awards and have remained in print for decades. He lives in Argyll.